"Lila, is Finn my son?" Mason asked.

Lila forced herself to look up into Mason's accusing eyes. She'd expected anger, knew she was deserving of it no matter her reasons for what she'd done, but the hurt she saw there nearly had her sinking to her knees. "Yes," she said with a soft sob.

Moisture flooded Mason's dark eyes as he stared down at her in disbelief. "I have a son."

"Mason…" she said, fear and regret threatening to swallow her up. "Finn doesn't know you're his father."

"I think that's pretty clear," he muttered with a deep-set frown. Dragging in a steadying breath, he ran a hand down his face and then pinned Lila with an accusatory gaze. "Why would you keep him from me? I loved you. I thought you loved me."

"I do," she countered with a hiccuping sob. "I…I mean I did." Admitting the truth would only set her up for more heartache, because the choices she'd made guaranteed Mason would never forgive her…

Kat Brookes is an award-winning author and past Romance Writers of America Golden Heart® Award finalist. She is married to her childhood sweetheart and has been blessed with two beautiful daughters. She loves writing stories that can both make you smile and touch your heart. Kat is represented by Michelle Grajkowski with 3 Seas Literary Agency. Read more about Kat and her upcoming releases at katbrookes.com. Email her at katbrookes@comcast.net. Facebook: Kat Brookes.

Books by Kat Brookes

Love Inspired

Small Town Sisterhood
With All Her Heart

Bent Creek Blessings
The Cowboy's Little Girl
The Rancher's Baby Surprise
Hometown Christmas Gift

Texas Sweethearts
Her Texas Hero
His Holiday Matchmaker
Their Second Chance Love

Visit the Author Profile page at Harlequin.com.

With All Her Heart

Kat Brookes

LOVE INSPIRED
INSPIRATIONAL ROMANCE

LOVE INSPIRED®
INSPIRATIONAL ROMANCE

ISBN-13: 978-1-335-55387-4

With All Her Heart

This edition published by arrangement with Harlequin Books S.A.

For questions and comments about the quality of this book, please contact us at CustomerService@Harlequin.com.

Love Inspired
22 Adelaide St. West, 40th Floor
Toronto, Ontario M5H 4E3, Canada
www.Harlequin.com

Printed in U.S.A.

The Lord is nigh unto all them that call
upon him, to all that call upon him in truth.
—*Psalms* 145:18

I'd like to dedicate this book to two women who, while not related by blood, are true sisters of my heart. Just as Lila and Addy are in this story. Missy Robinson and Cindy Duffy are my wonderful sisters-in-law. They've laughed with me. They've cried with me. We've spent the most amazing vacations together. I am so grateful to have them in my life.

Chapter One

The key will be under the flowerpot, where I've always kept it. Nothing's changed.

Lila Gleeson glanced at the screen of her cell phone, her stomach in knots as she reread Mama Tully's text message from that morning. That last statement couldn't be more wrong—everything in her life had changed since she'd left Sweet Springs, Georgia, some nine years ago. She was no longer the young girl who had been tossed about in the foster system, yearning so desperately for a family of her own, for the love she'd always been denied.

She was a grown woman of twenty-seven now. A single mother who, unlike her own parents, made certain her child knew just how very much he was loved. Eight-year-old Finn was her life's biggest blessing.

Her misty gaze lifted, once more taking in the charming old Victorian house that had been her home for three and a half years of her teenage life. It had been the first time she'd ever felt truly wanted. And, oh, how she'd missed Mama Tully. It had taken seven years to gather up the courage to contact her foster mother after she'd run off in the middle of the night, pregnant and guilt-ridden. This would be the first time she'd seen Mama Tully, as plans for her to visit Lila and Finn where they lived in Hillyer, Alabama, hadn't worked out as they had hoped.

The rear passenger door of her Jeep Cherokee opened. A second later, her son's dark head poked around the rear of the vehicle where she stood trying to tamp down the rush of emotion she felt at being back in Sweet Springs again. At being *home* again. "Should I take my backpack in with me?" he asked sleepily.

They had started out right after lunch, expecting a four-hour or so drive to Sweet Springs. Thanks to road construction they'd encountered along the way, and a late stop to stretch their legs and have dinner, they had arrived more than two hours behind schedule. Lila had called Mama Tully when they'd stopped for dinner along the way to check on her. But by the time they'd arrived at the hospital shortly before 7:00 p.m., Mama Tully had been sound asleep, recovering from her burst-appendix surgery and the subsequent peritonitis she'd suffered at just fifty years old. Lila had decided to let her sleep, leaving a message with the on-duty nurse that they would return the next morning.

Slipping her cell phone back into her purse, Lila smiled warmly at her son. "We won't be going anywhere else this evening, so you might as well take it inside with you."

"Okay," he said, disappearing around the side of the Jeep.

Emotion filled her when she thought about the choices she had made at seventeen, what that choice had taken from her son. Finn was her world. Just as his father had once been. She had tried so hard to set aside her memories of Mason Landers and the special times they had shared together. Tried to leave the past where it needed to be—in the past. But, apparently, love didn't work that way. It held firm, rooting deep. As did the regret of what might have been. She just prayed that time, along with what Mason must have seen as her betrayal of their love, had helped him to move on.

A part of that dream had been to follow in

his father's footsteps. Sharing the Lord's word with others as a preacher, which, according to a statement Mama Tully had made a few years before, was what exactly what Mason had been doing with his life. Not that Lila ever directly inquired about him. It was better not to, lest Mama Tully hear something in her voice that might give away Lila's heart's yearning for the boy she'd left behind. Man now, she mentally corrected herself, just as she was a grown woman.

Thankfully, Mason was thousands of miles away in Chile, sharing the word of God. Lila had learned that from Addy, her onetime foster sister and now her forever best friend. That was something Lila was pretty certain he might not have had the opportunity to do if she had remained in Sweet Springs after she'd found out she was carrying his child. People would have judged Mason for not practicing what he wanted to preach. His family, although incredibly kind and loving, would have been hurt deeply by the shame their son would have brought down upon them. Most especially Reverend Landers, Mason's father, who had sadly passed away a few years after Lila had left town.

She hadn't wanted to hurt any of them. They'd all been so good to her. She'd had to live with this choice for nine long years and would continue to do so for the rest of her life.

Sighing, Lila raised the rear lift gate of her SUV. Her son was busy gathering up the colored pencils and tablet he had entertained himself with for a good part of their trip. *Mason's* son. Finn was, at least according to her long-held memories and the wallet-size senior picture she'd taken with her the day she'd left Sweet Springs, the spitting image of the father he'd never known. Something that was both comforting and heartache inducing at the same time. It was as if Mason was still a part of her life, even though she had given him up a long time ago. Not because she'd wanted to. It was what she'd needed to do for all of them, and it had broken her heart.

Funny how life worked, she thought in reflection. Mason had left Sweet Springs to go off into the world and share the word with others, while she had just returned to the place that had once been her safe haven, so very distanced from the religion she had come to know during her time there as a teen. Lord knew she'd never intended to come home again, because that was what Sweet Springs had once been for her—*home*—but Addy hadn't been able to get the time off from her job to be there. So Lila had come in her stead, as she was off from school for summer break. She cherished that part of being a teacher, because it allowed her to spend more time with her son.

Overwhelmed by the flood of memories and resurfacing guilt, Lila fought the urge to get back in the car with her son and drive away. It was only her love and deep concern for her dear, sweet foster mother that kept her from doing just that. The memory of her foster mother and the unconditional love and support she had shown her over the years brought the burn of unshed tears to Lila's eyes. Not that Mama Tully had asked for any help. She was all about giving, never taking.

Lila had turned away from prayer years before, but she felt the unexpected urge to send an anxious plea heavenward. Not that she thought the Lord would be eager to receive any requests from someone who had turned her back on Him, giving up church and avoiding prayer because she felt so much guilt about everything that had happened. She had gotten pregnant outside the bonds of marriage, no matter how much she and Mason had loved each other; she experienced tremendous guilt because she had walked away from that love with a secret that had changed her entire life. Guilt for keeping Mason's son from him for all those years. But for the first time in what felt like forever, she truly felt the need to pray.

Lord, please give me strength as I prepare to face the life I gave up. A life I still long for, even after all these years.

Lila also knew she had to prepare herself for Mama Tully's reaction when she finally met Finn. A face she'd only seen in pictures. Ones Lila had specifically chosen, sending Mama Tully mostly faraway shots where her son's resemblance to Mason wasn't as noticeable. Probably a futile effort to guard the secret she'd kept for so many years, because Mama Tully of all people knew how deeply she'd felt about Mason.

It had taken seven of the nine years she had been away to gather up enough courage to make contact with her foster mother and try to mend fences. Mama Tully had planned to come visit them the previous July, but Finn had come down with chicken pox, which Mama Tully had never had, so she'd regretfully had to cancel her trip. They'd talked about her trying again, maybe over the holidays, but Honey and Grits had come along and things just hadn't worked out. So this visit would be their first meeting.

With a deep, fortifying breath, Lila began unloading their bags.

"How's it going up there?" she asked as she placed her suitcase onto the ground beside her.

"I packed everything away except for two pencils. They rolled off my seat," her son explained, his head dipping down as he bent to search for them.

"You can look for them tomorrow," she told him. It was late, and he was tired.

"But I need them to finish my picture."

Finn had been working diligently on a drawing of a sunlit sky over a field of flowers for Mama Tully. Something to brighten up her hospital room. "You can finish it in the morning before we leave for the hospital."

"Okay."

Lila sifted through their things to find Finn's suitcase. As she did so, she replayed the phone call she'd received from Addy in her mind. "Mrs. Landers called to let me know Mama Tully's sick, Lila," her best friend had said, her voice thick with emotion. And the hospital had made it clear that they couldn't release Mama Tully to go home unless she had someone there with her. So that would be Lila now and Addy as soon as she could arrange the time off work.

If only she had still been living in Sweet Springs, Lila thought regretfully, Mama Tully would never have waited so long to go to the hospital. Lila would have made certain of it. However, because of the life choices she had made at seventeen, she hadn't been there when her foster mother had needed her the most. And while they had worked toward mending their fences, there was still so much they needed to work through. That would have to wait, though, because her focus needed to be on getting Mama Tully better again.

She lowered her son's suitcase onto the gravel drive next to hers and then turned to look at the butter-yellow house with its dark green shutters and white trim. *Home.* Not that it was her home any longer, but that was what this place still felt like in her heart. The rightness of it made her want to weep.

"Ready," Finn said as he joined her behind the Jeep, his camo-print backpack strapped onto his back.

Grateful for her son's timing, as she needed to keep her emotions in check, she nodded. "Ready." Grabbing the raised handles of their suitcases, they started up the walkway leading to the old Victorian. As soon as they stepped foot onto the porch, excited barking erupted from somewhere inside.

"That must be Honey and Grits," Lila said, not missing the smile that spread like a wildfire across her son's face. Finn had always wanted a dog of his own. Unfortunately, their apartment complex didn't allow pets. This was his chance to experience what it would be like to have a dog—or in this case two—to care for.

According to Mama Tully, the dogs would be in capable hands until Lila could get there to take over, not that she needed to take on that responsibility. Lila had insisted otherwise. It was such a small thing to do for the woman who had done so much for her. Granted, Lila had no experience with animals of any kind. But, really, how hard could it be to feed and play with a couple of tailwagging pups?

Two very excitably *loud* pups. She hurried to retrieve the house key from under the flowerpot.

"Momma?" Finn said worriedly.

She glanced down, trying to force the past to the back of her memories. "Yes?"

"You look like you're fixing to cry."

With a sniffle, Lila shook her head and forced herself to pull it together as she met her son's worried gaze. "I'm just feeling a little emotional being back here again." It felt as though it were just yesterday that she'd stepped foot inside this old house. And yet, at times, it felt like a lifetime. In her son's case, it had been. He'd been conceived there in Sweet Springs but had spent his life away from what rightly should have been his home. Forcing that last thought aside, she unlocked the door and then swung it open.

The excited barking grew louder as they moved through the house to the back parlor with its open pocket doors. The entry had been partitioned off by a large expandable metal gate, behind which stood two dogs, barking in unison. A light breeze filtered into the house through a partially opened back window, causing the ruffles on the tie-back curtains that framed it to flutter ever so gently.

"I think they're happy to see us," her son exclaimed.

"I'm sure they're lonely here right now." She pointed to the larger of the two dogs, a beautiful black-and-white male Australian shepherd with mismatched eyes. "That must be Grits," she concluded, going by Mama Tully's description of her "babies." She pointed to the smaller dog. "And she must be Honey."

"Why are her legs so little?" Finn asked almost worriedly.

Lila laughed softly. "I believe they're supposed to be short like that. Honey's not the same kind of dog as Grits, even though they have similar coloring. Mama Tully said she's a corgi mix, and apparently they tend to have very short legs." She smiled down at the pup. "You are too cute."

The dog barked as if in agreement, and then both of Mama Tully's babies placed their front paws up on the gate, wagging their tails wildly. Lila reached down to give them each a soothing scratch behind the ear.

Finn did the same, his grin widening. Then he looked up at her. "Why are they named after food? It's silly."

A wistful smile moved over Lila's face. "They're named after Aunt Addy and me." Just as they did with Mama Tully, her son considered Addy family, too, blood related or not. Because Addy was the only one who knew the truth about Mason being Finn's daddy. Her foster sister had given Lila a place to stay when she was pregnant and then after she'd given birth to her son. She'd been a part of both her and Finn's lives ever since.

"But those aren't your names."

"No, they're not," she agreed. "But Gramma

Tully gave them names that reminded her of us. Honey for me, because after having my first taste of it after coming to live with her I would put it on almost everything I ate. Your aunt Addy, on the other hand, loved her grits. Cheese grits. Sausage grits. Fried grits. Just to name a few."

Grits ran to grab a bright red rubber ball that was lying in the far corner of the room and then ran back to the gate, shoving the toy at Finn. With a bark, Honey scampered over to snatch up a smaller pink ball, which she brought back with her. Then she sat, looking up at Finn with hopeful eyes.

Lila laughed. "I think they want to play." She unlatched the gate and stepped carefully through its narrow opening. They seemed friendly enough. Once she'd been happily greeted by the pair, tails enthusiastically wagging, she motioned for Finn to join her, making certain the dogs didn't slip out as he did so.

Honey and Grits dropped their balls and greeted Finn with eager, wet puppy kisses, nearly knocking him down with their enthusiastic welcome. Her son's boyish giggles filled the room.

Lila stood watching, soaking in the joy that came with her son's laughter. It was a balm to her aching soul. While her child was eager to finally meet the gramma he'd only spoken to on the phone—because Lila had been too afraid of Mama Tully guessing her long-kept secret were she to meet Finn in person—he'd also fretted over leaving Alabama at the start of summer break and missing out on all the fun his friends would be having. Maybe, just maybe, the pups would help to ease Finn's longing for his friends back home.

As she stood watching her son playing with the two dogs, she noted several near yawns, which he determinedly held at bay. Finn was tired and understandably so. "I think it's time for you to turn in for the night."

"But, Momma…" he groaned.

"It's been a long day," she told him. "And we'll be heading to the hospital in the morning. You'll have plenty of time to play with these two when we get back tomorrow," she said. "Now, let's go get you washed up and then into bed."

"Okay," he relented, sounding as tired as she herself felt.

Once that was done, she tucked her son into bed in what had once been Addy's bedroom. "I'll grab the rest of our things from the Jeep. Then I'll take Honey and Grits out for a short walk before I turn in for the night. Will you be okay in here?"

"Momma, I'm not a baby," he replied.

A tender smile moved across her face. "No, sweetie, you're not." Finn had lived in several places, so sleeping in a new bedroom wasn't as intimidating to him as it might be to other children. And knowing that it was his gramma Tully's house had to be comforting, as well. But she'd had to ask. Leaning in, she placed a good-night kiss on her son's brow. Then she straightened, wished him good-night once more and then started for the door.

"Don't forget to call Aunt Addy," Finn called after her.

She cast a smile back over her shoulder. "I won't. Hopefully she'll be able to free up some time to come join us here soon. 'Night, sweetie."

"'Night, Momma."

Turning off the overhead light, she left only the soft glow of the night-light on before pulling the door closed behind her and heading outside. Her thoughts went back to Mama Tully, hating the idea of her lying there all alone in that hospital room. She hoped they'd be able to bring Mama Tully home from the hospital very soon. It all depended on how quickly she recovered. However long it took, Lila would be there for her. School wouldn't be back in session until summer's end.

She paused at the edge of the porch, looking out, noting how big the shade trees in the front yard had gotten. Being back in Sweet Springs had stirred up so many emotions—happiness to be home again, longing for the life she'd once had and heartache at knowing the lie she had lived with for so many years would weigh even more heavily on her conscience with each passing day.

Lila drew to a stop at the edge of the porch, closed her eyes and breathed in the fresh country air. The mouthwatering scent of ripening peaches beckoned to her. She found herself moving toward it, cutting at an angle across the front yard in the direction of the orchard that edged that side of Mama Tully's property. Mason's family's orchard. Stopping just shy of the tree line, she closed her eyes once again and let the sweet fragrance of the plump, ready-for-picking fruits dotting the rows of trees wrap slowly around her, sweeping Lila's thoughts back to the past. To the time she'd spent among those trees with the boy who managed to find his way into her not-so-trusting heart. To Mason.

Mason Landers had decided to walk to Mrs. Tully's that evening to pick up Honey and Grits. He'd offered to see to his neighbor's dogs, along with her yardwork and garden, after she'd gone into the hospital. He would leave the dogs in their "playroom" during the day, making sure to stop by to let them out a time or two throughout the day while he was working in the orchard, his family's source of income. Then he would pick them up later in the afternoon to evening, after his work was done, and bring them back to his place to sleep.

He'd also felt the need to ask the Lord for peace where his heart was concerned. Spending so much time at his neighbor's place had evoked a lot of memories he'd forced aside years before. Memories of Lila. The girl he'd loved, had planned to spend his life with as husband and wife and had then lost, because she could never see how incredible she truly was. How lovable she was, even if her biological parents hadn't been able to show her because of their struggles with drug addiction.

He had spent a lot of evenings just like this one sitting on Mrs. Tully's front porch with Lila, looking up at the stars and talking about their hopes and dreams. Lila had been fostered there for a little over three years and had become so much more than a friend to Mason.

As he rounded the front of the house to

grab the spare house key Mrs. Tully kept tucked away under a flowerpot on her porch, Mason halted midstep. A woman stood with her back to him at the edge of the side yard, arms wrapped about herself as she stared off in the direction of his family's orchard.

"Can I help you?" he called out.

The woman jumped with a startled gasp.

"I didn't mean to..." he began, trailing off as she spun to face him. Mason's jaw dropped, and his heart, along with his feet, skidded to a halt. It had been years since he'd last seen her, but he would recognize that face anywhere.

"Mason?" she half squeaked, her sky blue eyes widening. Eyes that still lingered in his dreams along with Lila's infectiously bright smile. Not that she was doing any smiling right now. At that particular moment, she looked more like a deer caught up in the bright glow of a truck's headlights. Still, there was no denying that it was Lila Gleeson who stood in Mrs. Tully's front yard, staring back at him.

"Lila?" he heard himself say. He was just trying to process the fact that the girl he had once loved and had been loved by, the same girl who ran off without even a word of good-bye—unless one counted the brief note Lila

had left for him at the base of "their" tree—
was actually standing right there in front of
him. Same long, curly blond hair and strik-
ing blue eyes. Still petite in stature, but less
waiflike. Then again, she was no longer the
teenage girl he'd once been completely cow-
eyed over. The one he had so foolishly fallen
in love with, despite her constant pleading
for him in the beginning not to love her, telling him that she was unlovable. But he hadn't
given up on her and they'd fallen in love. He
believed that enough to buy an engagement
ring and begin planning how he would surprise her with his proposal of marriage. Only
he found out the hard way—Lila wasn't unlovable. She was just incapable of trusting her
heart completely to anyone.

"Y-you're back?" she stammered as if his
presence unnerved her. But then it might, seeing as how things had ended between them.

As his surprise at finding her there faded,
the resentment he had harbored threatened to
resurface. "Back?" he said, wanting to point
out that she was the one who had pulled up
stakes and left town all those years ago.

"I thought you were living in Chile."

"Where did you get that idea?" he asked.
"Sweet Springs is the only place I'll ever call
home."

"Of course, it is," she said, biting at her bottom lip as her attention shifted from him to Mama Tully's house behind him and then back again. "I meant that your momma told Addy you were living there on a mission trip when they spoke a month or so ago, so we thought—"

"Addy knew how to reach you?" he cut in.

As if realizing what she'd just revealed, Lila lowered her gaze. "Yes."

"Unbelievable," he muttered under his breath. Addy and his mother talked every so often, but she had never once let on to any of them that she knew where Lila was. And it hadn't crossed his mind that she might be keeping Lila's whereabouts from them. If she'd left both Mrs. Tully and him without a word of where she was going, why would he think Lila would have done otherwise with her? His mistake had been assuming that if anyone knew where Lila was they would have made mention of it. Addy had to have known how Lila's leaving had affected them all. "Well, you and Addy thought wrong. Why are you here anyway?"

"I came to be here for Mama Tully, to care for her after she gets home. At least, until Addy gets here to take over."

"Apparently, Addy, through my mother, has

filled you in on everything that's happened in regard to Mrs. Tully," he remarked with a frown.

"Yes."

"Then you're also aware that Mrs. Tully nearly died. Yet, here you are, back in Sweet Springs. Have you given any thought to what the shock of seeing you after all these years, without any warning whatsoever, could do to her?"

Her teary gaze lifted to meet his. "She knows I'm here."

"She knows?" That made no sense. He and Mrs. Tully had both grieved over Lila's leaving. Prayed for her to have a change of heart and come back to them safe and sound. After that first year, they'd stopped talking about her. It had become too painful to them both. "So Mrs. Tully has been in contact with you, too?"

"For a little less than two years," she admitted. "It took me that long to gather up the courage to contact her."

To contact Mrs. Tully, but not him. The man she'd said she loved and had talked about marrying someday. Jaw clenched at the betrayal he felt for so many reasons, Mason said, "Getting back to your question, I returned home a couple of weeks ago. Because that's what Sweet Springs will always be to me—my home. Not that I'd expect you to understand that. Home seems to have a completely different meaning for you. Something more temporary with no emotional commitments." His words were harsh, but Mason couldn't bring himself to regret them. They'd come from his heart. A heart that had been left battered by her betrayal of their friendship. Of their love.

Tears pooled in her eyes. "I suppose I deserved that."

His father had given so many sermons over the years on forgiveness, but at that moment Mason couldn't seem to recall the particulars of any of them. All he could think about was what Lila had done to him, to all those who had cared about her, when she'd run away. He wanted to demand to know where she'd gone to, not that she owed him any answers. He had searched for Lila for months on end after she'd gone, scanning the faces of every person he saw in every town he went to. He made the mistake at that moment of looking into those big blue tear-filled eyes, and guilt he didn't want to feel shoved his anger aside.

"No," he relented with a heavy sigh, "you didn't. I shouldn't have said what I did."

"I know that I hurt you—" she began.

"I was young," he said, cutting off the apology he guessed was about to come. He didn't want or need it. "We both were," he added, trying to temper his words. "Those foolish notions I had in my head as a young boy are long gone."

Liar! his heart countered as he said aloud, "As far as I'm concerned, the past is where it belongs, leaving me free to live my life without any of the complications a relationship can bring."

She looked up at him in pained silence for several long moments before nodding in agreement.

Mason shook his head, frustration filling him. Much to his dismay, she'd become even more beautiful with the passing of time. "Lila, why are you here? You certainly haven't made any attempts to visit before this. Why now?" He folded his arms across his chest, as if doing so would keep his pounding heart from beating its way right through his rib cage. He longed to have answers to all the questions that had taken up permanent residence in his mind in the months, even years, since. But that had been a long time ago. He'd turned his focus to getting his business degree and implementing changes to the family market and orchards, doing his best to move on. Not that thoughts of Lila, both good and bad, hadn't still crept in from time to time, but he'd done his best to shove any lingering feelings he had for the woman standing before him aside.

She shifted uneasily from one foot to the other, her gaze drifting again in the direction of the house, as if deciding whether or not to make a run for it. It wouldn't surprise him if she did.

"As you've already pointed out, Mama Tully almost died," she said woefully. "When Addy called to tell me that Mama Tully had taken ill and that she couldn't get the time off work to come here right away, I knew I needed to do whatever I could to help her as she recovers."

He still couldn't believe she was there. After all these years. "Just how long has Addy known how to reach you?" he asked, feeling the fool.

Lila's lips pressed together in a grimace before she finally replied, "Since right after I left Sweet Springs."

He turned away, dragging a hand back through the thick, wavy strands of his dark hair. Why hadn't he thought to get ahold of Addy and press her for information about Lila's whereabouts? If he had, then maybe they could have worked through whatever it was. Maybe they would have still had a chance to have that future together they had talked about so often. And why did any of that matter now anyway? He knew why. Because a part of his heart still hadn't let go.

"Please don't be upset with Addy," Lila pleaded. "She didn't know about my leaving Sweet Springs until I showed up on her doorstep. I made her promise not to say anything to anyone."

"Well, you might have at least let Mrs. Tully know that you were safe instead of waiting years to do so. You weren't even eighteen," he said. It didn't matter that she would have been on her birthday the week after she'd left town. She was still underage and that caused everyone to worry after her. "She was half out of her mind after you'd gone. Filled with fear that something bad might happen to you. Did you know that? Not to mention buried in guilt, wondering what it was she had done to send you running away."

Tears spilled down Lila's cheeks, and it was all Mason could do not to wrap his arms around her. "She didn't do anything. I told her as much in the letter I left her. I wanted her to know that she was the mother I had always dreamed of having and that I would never forget her."

Unlike Mrs. Tully, he hadn't received a letter telling him how much he'd meant to her. His letter, brief as it had been, had consisted of Lila apologizing for leaving the way she had and saying that she wanted him to be happy, something her being in his life could never bring him. As far as he was concerned, he should have been the one to decide whether or not they could be happy together. That was what had been the catalyst for her leaving. Or had it been?

"In the letter you left me," he said, unable to keep the question bottled up inside him any longer, "you said you were leaving because you couldn't make me happy. And since I know that's far from the truth, I have to ask, is it because of what happened between us that day?" He didn't have to specify what day. They both knew what he was referring to. The day he had allowed the comfort he sought to give her following the unexpected news of her birth parents' deaths due to overdoses to turn into something else. He should have been strong enough to stop things before they went too far between the two of them. It didn't matter that he'd loved Lila with all of his heart. That he'd intended to ask her to marry him, to wear the ring he'd intended to surprise her with on her eighteenth birthday until they'd finished college and could begin their lives together as husband and wife.

What they'd done that day had changed things between them. They both knew they had sinned. But while he knew that sins could be forgiven, Lila hadn't seemed to be able to forgive herself, which had her distancing herself from not only him but the Lord, as well. She stopped going to church, making up excuses as to why she couldn't go, and then began pushing him away emotionally. Before he could figure out a way to set things right between them, she was gone.

"Mason," she said with unexpected tenderness, "you and I both know neither of us were prepared for what happened between us. And we both know it was wrong in God's eyes. I know because I saw the guilt there every time I looked into yours. Felt it myself."

"It was wrong," he agreed, "but at the same time, it was right. I cared for you, Lila." More than she would ever know.

"And I cared for you," she said with a regretful smile. Sadness filled her eyes. "I was so sorry to hear about your daddy's passing. I wish I could have been here for you."

"But you weren't," he stated, hating the

hurt he heard in his voice when he spoke. "In fact," he said, "you were long gone by then." His father had died from an undiagnosed heart condition a few years after Lila had gone. When he hadn't returned from his church meeting, and hadn't returned any of their mother's calls, Mason and his younger brother, Jake, had offered to go check on him while their momma and Mason's younger sister, Violet, continued making peach preserves to sell at their family fruit market. Mason and Jake had found him. He thanked the Lord every day that their mother hadn't gone with them that day. That was not the last memory he wanted her to have of her husband.

"Addy didn't find out about your daddy's passing until a week after his funeral. If I had known..." she said sorrowfully, eyes shimmering with unshed tears.

"What?" he scoffed, not wanting to talk about his father. Not wanting to talk about what she might have done when he knew better. "You would have come home?"

Her gaze dropped once more.

"I didn't think so." Distracted by the mention of his father's passing, Mason nearly let her other words slide by. She wasn't going to be the reason he gave up on his dream. That, and the shame their youthful indiscretion was why she had left all those years ago? Why hadn't Lila come to him about her concerns? They'd talked about everything else, including her painful past and the insecurities it had left residing within her. Some of his anger left him. "You shouldn't have given up the home you'd found for my sake. I didn't need protecting, Lila. I would have faced up to what I'd done and set things right."

She dragged her gaze back up to meet his. "Mason…"

"Dreams change, Lila. While I admit there was a time when I truly considered following in my daddy's footsteps, a man whose dedication to the Lord and his congregation, even his family, was given wholeheartedly, I came to the realization in college that his calling was not the same as mine." He motioned toward the fruit-laden trees beside them. "Mine was to work this land. To carry on what my granddaddy started here all those years ago. I ended up switching my major from theology to business and have focused on growing the family orchard and market sale ever since. Although I still devote some of my time to going on mission trips in honor of Daddy."

"I'm glad you're doing what makes you happy," she told him, her gaze moving in the direction of the fruit trees. "It looks like you made the right decision. The orchard looks more bountiful than I remember."

"It is," he replied. "We updated the irrigation system, and Jake and I have been testing out a newer fertilizer. The crops have been responding well to it."

"I'll bet your momma is beyond thrilled to have even more peaches to do wondrous things with." She grew serious. "How is she doing?"

The pain of his father's loss still cut deep for him. He remembered how hard it had been to deal with the grief—without Lila. He could have turned to his family, but they'd had enough of their own hurt heaped onto their emotional plates without him adding to it. He'd gotten through it. As his mother liked to point out, the Landerses were made of strong Southern stock. They could get through anything.

"She stays busy," he answered, grateful that his mother had the family fruit market and bakery to keep her occupied.

"Addy said you renovated the market."

"We did," he acknowledged with a nod. "I drew up plans, and then Jake and I added on to the building, opening it up into one large commercial area to sell peaches and baked goods."

Mason had always had a gift for creating ideas on paper. "It sounds so nice. I'm sure your momma loves it."

"She does. The new layout makes it easier for her to check customers out at one register rather than running back and forth from the market to the bakery when Violet isn't able to help out." The Perfect Peach was twice the size it had once been, his mother's pride and joy, and boasted a large selection of related items, such as lotions with peach extract, scented candles, T-shirts—you name it.

"I'm glad she has you all to lean on."

You could have had me to lean on, too, he thought bitterly. "That's what families do," he said, then regretted his comment when he saw the sadness that filled her pretty bright blue eyes. Lila had never had a family of her own. Mrs. Tully had been the closest thing she'd ever had. Even after moving to Sweet Springs, Lila had still clung to hope that her mother and father would get the help they needed that would allow them to finally be a real family. When they'd died, it had broken her emotionally.

And it had been his efforts to draw her back from that dark place, his need to comfort her and take away the pain, that had drawn them both down the wrong path. Not that he hadn't loved Lila—he had—but they should have been older. They should have been married.

Her wounded gaze strayed to the house and then back to him, this time not quite meeting his. "I should go get the rest of my things. It was nice seeing you again." She started past him in the direction of what must have been her Jeep.

"Do you really think staying here is a good idea?"

Lila stopped and turned to look at him. "I know you'd probably prefer otherwise, but I need to be here. Even more so when Mama Tully comes home, which I hope will be very soon."

"Her doctor says it could be another week or longer," he explained. His mother had been visiting Mrs. Tully that morning when her doctor came in to check on her. Peritonitis had set in after her appendix burst, requiring not only the removal of the organ but also to eliminate the infection and avoid sepsis, meaning an even longer recovery time.

"Well, that will give me plenty of time to see to it that Mama Tully's house is in tip-top shape before she gets home. She's going to need to rest and not fuss over sweeping and dusting and whatnot. Oh, and I'll need to tend to her vegetable garden. And—"

"That's my job," he cut in.

She lifted her gaze to his. "Excuse me?"

"I take it Mrs. Tully didn't think to mention that I'm looking after her place while she's in the hospital?"

"If she had, I wouldn't have been so shocked to see you," she pointed out. "If you recall, I thought you were out of the country. Actually, she never mentioned any names, just that the dogs were being cared for until I could get here to look after them."

"I recall," he replied. "You're welcome to do any housekeeping you think needs done, and take over with Honey and Grits, but I'll be seeing to the yardwork and garden as promised. Which, of course, means we're bound to cross paths if you plan on staying here. Are you going to be okay with that?"

She hesitated at that and then said, "I'm sure Mama Tully appreciates the help you've been able to give her, but I'm perfectly capable of mowing her grass and weeding her vegetable garden as well while I'm staying here."

Oh, how the set of her jaw brought back memories of the Lila who had first come to live in Sweet Springs. They'd met in the summer in his family orchard. He'd been out walking and had come across Lila sitting beneath one of the peach trees, writing in her journal. She'd been defensive, stubborn, with emotional walls that were sky-high. She'd let down her guard around him over time, trusting him, confiding in him. Yet, she had always remained determined not to let anyone else do something for her she could do for herself.

That apparently hadn't altered any. Not that he planned to try. The less interaction he had with her, the better, as far as he was concerned. She could see to her commitments to Mrs. Tully and he would see to his. Or Lila could make the whole situation far less complicated and go back to wherever it was she'd come from. He and his family could see to Mrs. Tully when she came home. Even as that option settled in his mind, another part of him—his contrary heart, to be precise— jumped for joy inside his chest at the thought of Lila sticking around.

"Until I hear differently from Mrs. Tully, I'll still be stopping by to see to the responsibilities I've taken on here."

"Mason," she pleaded.

"Lila," he countered evenly. He wondered whatever he could be thinking, falling into this battle of wills with Lila.

"Fine," Lila said before he could reconsider his stance on the matter and relinquish responsibility to her. "You take care of the grounds, and I'll see to the pups. I think it would be best, however, if we set a scheduled time for you to come by. Or you could call before stopping by."

"If that will help you sleep at night," he countered with a nonchalant shrug, as if her wanting to be anywhere but where he was didn't jab at a part of his heart he'd thought permanently numbed. "Jake and I usually make our rounds through the orchards in the mornings, sometimes into the first part of the afternoon. I'll do my best to stop by here, say, at three or four every afternoon. Feel free to go into town or stay in the house while I'm here. It makes no difference to me." It was probably for the best he hadn't gone into preaching, because that was far from true.

"That works for us," Lila muttered. "Now, if you'll excuse me, I really need to finish unpacking the car."

"Us?" His gaze shifted immediately to the old Victorian. Someone had come with her? A husband? The second that possibility arose in his mind, he felt an even stronger stirring of emotion. Jealousy? The last thing he should be feeling, considering Lila was not his girl. Hadn't been for nearly a decade. She wasn't even a girl anymore. She was a woman. A stranger behind that beautiful face he'd never forgotten. Lord knew, he wasn't emotionally prepared to deal with any of this. But deal with it he would. Maybe once he'd had time to let things sink in, time to work through the maelstrom of emotions seeing Lila again had stirred up inside him, he'd be better prepared to cope.

"Us," she repeated, casting an anxious glance toward the old house. "I was referring to the dogs and myself."

He exhaled the breath he hadn't even realized he was holding, then muttered with a frown, "Well, then, I'd best make myself scarce." Turning away, he started into the orchard, pausing to glance back over his shoulder at her. "Just so you know, I could have been happy with you." That said, he walked away.

Chapter Two

❧

Lila poked her head into the hospital room the next day, only to discover Mama Tully sleeping peacefully. Blessedly, no pain was etched into the older woman's still youthful, though slightly pale, face. Her heart swelled with happiness at seeing her beloved foster mother again after so many years. There was so much she wanted to say. So much she wanted to tell her. So much she could never share. There would be time for all of that once Mama Tully was well. For now, she needed to rest.

"She's sleeping." Lila turned to whisper to her son.

Finn, who had been standing behind her, peered around Lila, his gaze going first to Mama Tully and then to the monitor positioned next to her hospital bed with all its flashing lights and numbers. With an unexpected sob, he backed out of the room and darted down the hallway.

Lila hurried after him, calling out his name. She found him standing at the end of the corridor, peering out of the oversize window that looked out over the parking lot outside. He clenched the picture he'd drawn for Mama Tully tightly in his tiny hand. She closed the distance between them. "Sweetie…"

He looked back over his shoulder, unshed tears looming in his dark brown eyes. *Mason's eyes.*

She knelt in front of him and reached out to cup his cheek. "Honey, what's wrong?"

"I don't want Gramma Tully to die before she gets to meet me."

Her heart squeezed at the fear she heard in her son's voice. Although Finn had spoken to Mama Tully over the phone many times since Lila finally told her foster mother that she had a son, they had never met in person. Mama Tully never left Sweet Springs, and Lila had told her she couldn't bring herself to face the past she'd left behind. It was the truth. Mama Tully had opened her always loving heart up to Finn. Had even insisted that he call her Gramma Tully. Lila had also sent Mama Tully pictures of her and Finn, mostly faraway shots to lessen the chance of her foster mother discovering out the truth.

So they'd settled for keeping up with each other's lives through phone calls. Another blessing was that Mama Tully was not a fan of technology. Had she been, there was a chance she would have wanted to video chat with Finn and realized who the boy's father was.

"She's not going to die," Lila assured her son. She couldn't. Mama Tully was far too young, far too kind, to be taken away in the prime of her life. Surely that wasn't in God's plan for her, or He wouldn't have given Lila a second chance. She prayed not. There were too many emotional fences she needed to mend. And her adorably affectionate dogs needed her, as Lila and Addy had once needed their emotional rock when no one else wanted to care for them. "She's just tired," she told him with a tender smile.

His gaze drifted past her down the hallway and then back to Lila, a deep frown etched in his face. "I don't like all those machines."

"I know they might seem a little scary at first, but they are there to help the patients who are staying here get better," she explained. Her son had never been in a hospital room before, so his trepidation was understandable. They'd only gone as far as the nurses' station the day before when they were told Mama Tully was sleeping, and Lila had decided it was best to wait to see her, not wanting to interrupt her rest. She wished that she had thought to prepare Finn better, but her thoughts had been all in a tangle over her unexpected run-in with Mason the evening before. It had been one of the hardest things she'd ever done, and she'd experienced more than enough heartache in her lifetime.

Straightening, she held out her hand with a smile. "Are we going back to Gramma Tully's house?" her son asked as he took hold of it.

She shook her head. "No. I would imagine she's just taking a short nap. We'll just sit quietly until she wakes," she told him as they made their way back to Mama Tully's hospital room. "Maybe you can draw her another picture while we wait."

"Okay," Finn murmured, slightly distracted by all the commotion going on around them. Nurses scurrying in and out of doorways. The sound of medical equipment beeping in the nearby rooms as it filtered out into the narrow corridor. The occasional announcement made on the PA system echoed along the hallway.

This time, when they entered the room, Finn following behind her, Mama Tully was awake, sitting nearly upright, her back and head propped against a pillow.

"As I live and breathe, Lila!" she exclaimed the moment she saw her in the doorway. Her voice, though slightly hoarse from sleep, was filled with more exuberance than Lila would have expected possible.

"Mama Tully!" she exclaimed, joy squeezing her heart as she crossed the room. "I wasn't sure you'd recognize me."

The older woman laughed, and then said with a teasing grin, "They removed my appendix. Not my memory. I'd know that pretty face anywhere." She opened her arms wide in welcome.

Lila leaned in over the side of the hospital bed to return the offered hug. Then she straightened, looking down at her foster mother with tear-blurred eyes. "I've been so worried about you."

Mama Tully smiled up at her. "I'm a tough old bird. Takes more than an ornery appendix and a little infection to keep me down."

At just over fifty years old, she was hardly an old bird. But she was tough. Mama Tully had survived the loss of her husband at a very young age, had singlehandedly taken on the raising of two young, somewhat troubled foster girls and had built a life for herself.

Thankfully, her husband, a few years older than Mama Tully, had thought to invest in life insurance, which included a policy that paid off the house should he pass away. She'd also received a small monthly income during her years as a foster parent, which she put toward Lila's and Addy's needs before placing the rest in the bank for, in her words, a rainy day.

Lila returned her smile and then turned to her son, who stood a few feet behind her. "It's all right, sweetie," she assured him once more and then motioned for him to join them. "Come on over and say hello."

Mama Tully was visibly unable to contain her joy when Finn stepped forward to greet her with a "Hello, Gramma Tully. I'm Finn."

"Hello, Finn," Mama Tully said, her voice choked. "I don't suppose you might have brought a hug for me."

He glanced down at the IV taped to the back of Mama Tully's hand, worry creasing his tiny brow.

"This is how they give me some of my medicines," she explained. "We just have to be careful this tube doesn't get pulled on too hard."

He frowned. "I don't want to hurt you."

"Bless your heart," she said, her expression tender. "You're not going to hurt me. They have this little tube taped onto my hand very securely."

Lila was grateful Mama Tully hadn't mentioned the IV having been inserted into her vein. Finn was skittish enough about this hospital visit. "You can give Gramma Tully an easy hug. Like you give Peaches when we visit Aunt Addy." Peaches was Addy's orange-and-white tabby cat, a former stray.

Finn set his drawing on the nearby chair and then scooted closer to the bed. Leaning in, he hugged Mama Tully. "I'm glad you're okay," he said as she wrapped her loving arms around him.

"So am I," she said, her voice filled with emotion. "But if this is what it took to bring you and your momma back to Sweet Springs, I would go through it all over again." And then the tears came.

Seeing the overwhelming joy that meeting Finn had brought to Mama Tully was all it took to burst the dam of emotion Lila had been holding back. Tears came by the bucketful from both women. After bawling her eyes out the night before following her heart-tugging run-in with Mason, Lila was surprised she had any tears left to cry. But there they were.

Mama Tully released Finn with a sniffle

and then took a moment to regain her composure.

Finn stood looking between the two teary-eyed women.

"Don't mind your momma and I," Mama Tully told him as she reached for the miniature box of tissues on her bedside table. She handed a tissue to Lila and then plucked one out for herself. "Women tend to cry a lot when we're happy."

He looked up at Lila. "Is that why you were crying last night? 'Cause you were happy to be back?"

He'd heard her? *Oh, Finn.*

Mama Tully's gaze shifted to Lila.

"Coming back stirred up a lot of memories for me," she admitted as she stood looking down into Mama Tully's always kind eyes. Knowing eyes. Eyes that held the questions Mama Tully had tried to ask in the beginning, ones that Lila had immediately steered away from. Mama Tully hadn't pressed anymore, no doubt fearing Lila's pushing her away again.

Lila turned to her son. "Yes, Finn, I am very happy to be back." Or at least a part of her was. The other part of her dreaded running into Mason and once again seeing the resentment and hurt in his eyes. She'd come so close to telling him about Finn. But she'd caused him enough hurt as it was.

Mama Tully offered her an empathetic smile. "I'm sure it has. But I feel like my prayers have finally been answered, having you here." She looked to Finn. "Both of you."

"Finn, sweetie," Lila said, "don't you have something you wanted to give Gramma Tully?"

"I do," he said, grinning wide, then lifted the drawing he'd done for her and placed it atop the crisp white bedsheet that covered Mama Tully's lap.

She studied the picture before lifting her gaze to Finn, who stood eagerly watching for her reaction to his artwork. "You did this?"

He nodded proudly. "It's my family." Reaching out, he pointed to each of the people he'd drawn standing next to the house. "That's Momma and then you. This is Aunt Addy. She's holding Peaches, her kitty." His finger slid over to the edge of the house's porch, where two dogs lay beside two bright red balls. "That's—"

"Honey and Grits," Mama Tully finished for him, her eyes tearing up once again. "I think this is the nicest gift I've ever received."

"He certainly doesn't get his creativeness from me," Lila said without thinking. The last thing she wanted to do was stir up questions about Finn's supposed father. Her son had only recently begun asking questions about his father, no longer satisfied by her telling him that families weren't always made up of mommas and daddies and their children.

"Sometimes talent is just plain God-given," Mama Tully said, looking to Lila. "Now, tell me about my babies. How are they faring with me away?" she asked, thankfully redirecting the focus of their conversation.

Lila gave her a grateful smile.

"They like to play ball," Finn answered excitedly.

"Especially Grits," Lila chimed in. "His energy is endless."

"He likes to bite my feet."

Mama Tully's eyes widened worriedly. "He bit you?"

"More of a playful nip," Lila corrected. "And only at our heels when we're walking away."

Relief eased her features. "It's common for Australian shepherds to try and herd you as they would sheep or cattle." Her expression turned fretful once more. "I do hope they're not too much for you. I know you aren't used to having dogs of any kind underfoot. If they are, I'll ask Mason to continue looking after them. He's been watching over things for me while I've been in the hospital." Her expression suddenly changed, concern replacing her smile. "Oh no. I meant to call Mason yesterday, after I knew you were definitely coming, to let him know. But I was so tired, as you know, and completely forgot."

"We ran into each other last night," Lila told her, trying not to let the effect that meeting had had on her show. Mama Tully would only worry over her.

"Who's Mason?" her son asked, looking up at Lila.

"He was a very good friend of your momma's when she lived in Sweet Springs. He and his family live next door to your gramma Tully." She looked to Lila. "It must have been such a shock for him, finding you there. I thought it best not to mention it to him, since you had no plans to return to Sweet Springs—until now. I pray things weren't too awkward between the two of you."

It was all Lila could do not to look to her son, who was living, breathing proof of that past. But to do so would possibly lead Mama Tully to put two and two together, something she'd thankfully hadn't done. Maybe the resemblance between Finn and his father was more in her mind than what others saw in person.

"It was a little awkward," Lila admitted. *More than a little*, she thought to herself, having had to face his less-than-warm welcome. Face the future she had run away from. Face the painful realization that he truly had moved on. Those things had hurt so deeply, but she knew now that she had made the right decision in leaving all those years ago. And if she and Mason both stuck to their settled-upon agreement, neither of them would have to go through the discomfort again.

Mama Tully fretted. "I'm sorry, honey. If being at the house and crossing paths with Mason is going to be too uncomfortable for you—"

"It's not," Lila told her, not wanting Mama Tully to worry about any sort of conflict arising between her and Mason. "Mason and I are both adults, and our focus is on taking any and all burdens—or blessings, as in the case of Honey and Grits—off your shoulders until you are recovered enough to see to them yourself. He'll see to the yardwork and garden, and I'll care for your babies while I'm here."

"Those two can be a little ornery at times," Mama Tully said worriedly. "I hope they don't get to be too much."

Lila gave her a reassuring smile. "You needn't worry yourself about that. Your babies are no trouble at all." Mason living right next door, however, was a whole different story.

* * *

"Mason?"

Releasing his hold on the bushel of peaches he'd just set down next to the bakery counter, Mason straightened. He turned to find his sister, Violet, looking at him as if he'd put his shirt on backward that morning.

"What?"

"Are you feeling all right?" she asked with a frown.

"Never been better," he answered absently as he started past her. He had work to do and wasn't exactly feeling social that afternoon.

"Mason," she said insistently, causing him to stop midstride and turn to face her. Her expression was one of concern. "What's going on with you? You haven't been yourself the past few days."

"What makes you think—"

"I found him." They turned to face Jake, who was moving toward them, cell phone pressed to his ear, gaze fixed on Mason.

Him? With Violet being the only other person in the vicinity, Mason deduced his younger brother was referring to him. "I didn't realize I was lost," Mason said in an attempt at humor. Jake ended his call and shoved his cell phone back into the pocket of his jeans.

"Lost *and* confused, apparently," his little sister remarked, pointing at the bushel of peaches Mason had just carried in from the orchard.

Looking down, Mason gave himself a mental head shake, his sister's concern suddenly making sense. He'd delivered the additional peaches his mother had requested for the market's bakery to the wrong place. Frowning, he retraced his steps to retrieve the round wooden basket. When he turned, he found himself hemmed in by his brother and sister, who were standing side by side, arms crossed, blocking the direct route to the market's exit.

"Momma's waiting," he told them.

"And so are we," his sister announced determinedly.

His younger brother nodded. "Waiting for you to tell us what's had you so distracted."

"Can it wait until I get these to Momma?"

They didn't budge.

Mason sighed. He supposed they were bound to find out sooner or later. Word traveled fast in small towns. "Lila's back. I ran into her a few days ago, over at Mrs. Tully's place."

Their stubborn expressions turned to shock.

"Your Lila?" Jake gasped.

"She's not mine," Mason muttered in irritation. Never was. He'd just been too blinded by young love to see that for himself.

"What is she doing here?" his sister demanded with a frown. "If she thinks she's going to be welcomed back with open arms, she's got another think coming."

Unlike Lila, his family was loyal to a fault. *I wasn't going to be the reason you gave up your dream, your family's dream for you.* Had she truly left because she thought his being with her would hold him back from becoming whatever it was he would choose to become? Or was that another one of her convenient sidesteps from the truth—that she had never truly loved him the way he had loved her?

"I don't think she expects anything," he admitted. "Lila is here for Mrs. Tully. She's going to be watching over her dogs while she's in the hospital, and then see to Mrs. Tully herself once she gets home."

"Mrs. Tully's done fine without Lila's help all these years," his sister wasted no time in pointing out. Although she'd been just shy of fourteen at the time, Violet knew how deeply Lila's departure had hurt him.

"True," Mason agreed with a nod, "but the hospital will only release her into somebody's care."

"There are plenty of people here in Sweet Springs who would be willing to help out until Mrs. Tully is back on her feet again."

"I agree. But it's not our decision to make."

"I thought you were seeing to Honey and Grits," Jake chimed in.

Mason looked to his younger brother. "I was, but now Lila is here to look after them."

"For how long?"

"I don't know," he admitted with a shrug. "Long enough to get Mrs. Tully home and back on her feet again."

Confusion knit his brother's brows together. "How did Lila even know Mrs. Tully was in the hospital?"

"Addy told her," Mason replied.

"Addy?" Jake repeated in surprise. "She knew how to reach Lila?"

Mason's frown deepened. "From the start, according to Lila."

"How could she keep something like that from us?" Violet demanded. "She knew how upset we all were after Lila had gone. She could have said something to Momma during any one of their phone conversations over the years."

"Should have," his brother grumbled with a scowl.

"Lila made her promise not to," Mason said in Addy's defense. Not that her silence sat well with him, but she wasn't there to defend her actions. "You and Violet would have done the same for me if I had asked you to keep a secret."

"But we're family," she argued.

"Lila and Addy might not be blood related, but they were foster sisters," he reminded them.

"I can't believe you didn't tell us Lila was back," his sister said with an accusatory glance.

"Yeah," Jake agreed.

"No reason to," he told them. "As far as I'm concerned, her being here isn't going to affect my life."

His younger brother quirked a dark brow. "I'd say it already has."

"It won't again," Mason assured them as he tightened his grip on the misdelivered basket of peaches. Once he was over the shock of seeing her again, everything would be all right. At least, he prayed it would. Because contrary to what he'd said about Lila not affecting his life, she had. Her return had affected his sleep, his ability to focus and, to his frustration, his emotional state. It had to stop.

"I've got to get these over to the house," he said, stepping around the barricade his siblings had formed with their bodies. "Momma's waiting."

A little over an hour later, Mason climbed into his Gator, the utility vehicle he used at times to get around the orchard, and headed off through the peach-dappled trees toward Mrs. Tully's place. It was ten minutes past three o'clock, falling within the time frame he and Lila had agreed upon in order to avoid crossing paths with each other, and she was most likely at the hospital.

His momma seemed to be the only one in his family oblivious to his inner turmoil. But then she'd been distracted by the onslaught of pie orders every harvest season brought in.

"It's been nine years," he muttered to himself. "Let it go." *Let her go.*

Most days he avoided giving any thought to the old peach tree where he and Lila used to meet after school. A place where she'd once trusted him enough to share her painful past with him. A place where she used to go to sit and write her innermost thoughts down in her private journal. A place where their friendship had blossomed, apparently more deeply for him than for her. But since their encounter days before, all those memories had resurfaced, beckoning him to that spot.

Maybe he needed to go there. Needed to be reminded of the hurt Lila had caused him. Of the hole her leaving town had left in his heart. Something to help steel his emotions for the times that they would inadvertently cross paths. Sweet Springs was a small town. It was almost unavoidable. He just prayed her stay wouldn't be a long one and that he could go back to his blessedly uncomplicated life. *Blessedly lonely*, his heart chimed in with the unwanted reminder. Sure, there had been opportunities to go out with other women over the years, but he wasn't the kind of man to lead someone on. His heart wasn't available for the giving, maybe never would be again.

Mason shoved that thought away, turning his focus instead to the peaches that hung heavy on the carefully pruned branches around him. That particular section would be harvested within the next several days, providing him a much-needed distraction. Something to focus on instead of his temporary neighbor who had, much to his chagrin, grown even prettier with time.

He eased his foot up on the Gator's gas pedal as he neared *the* tree, and thankfully so, because Grits suddenly darted out from between two trees on his left, coming to a stop the moment he caught sight of the utility vehicle. Mason did the same, slamming his booted foot down onto the utility vehicle's brake pedal.

So this was how Lila dog sat? Turning them loose to run wild? He glanced about for Honey, who was always trailing after her sidekick.

"Grits!"

Both Mason and the dog, tongue lolling out from its run, turned their heads in the direction the voice had come from. Before he could register the fact that it wasn't Lila in pursuit of Mrs. Tully's Australian shepherd, a young boy emerged past what used to be his and Lila's special tree.

The dog barked, and the boy turned, his frantic expression sliding instantly away.

"There you are!" he said, relief clear in his voice. And then, as if just noticing Mason, who was still seated nearby inside his utility vehicle, he swung his gaze around.

Confusion left Mason speechless for several long moments. Where had this kid come from? Who was he?

"Hello," the boy said with a smile that seemed so familiar.

"Hello," Mason managed, but before he could utter another word, Grits darted off into the orchard in the opposite direction from which he'd come.

Panic lit the kid's face.

"Finn!" an achingly familiar voice called out from somewhere beyond in the orchard.

"Mom!"

Mason was gutted by the sudden realization of who this boy was. As if to verify his conclusion, Lila burst through the tree line, her long blond curls bouncing wildly about her shoulders and down her back. Her gaze lit on her son first, and then, catching sight of Mason in her peripheral vision, she came to an immediate, stumbling stop. The long red leash she held in one hand swung to and fro as she fought to regain her balance.

"Mason," she said with a gasp.

As he stood staring at Lila, all he could think about was the fact that this pint-size bright-eyed boy with his short, dark curls—curls he'd clearly inherited from his mother—must be Lila's son.

"I…" she began, as if struggling for words.

Several excited barks erupted from deeper in the orchard.

"Mom," her son said anxiously.

"I'll get him," Mason said, cutting the engine. Exiting the Gator, he closed the distance between Lila and himself and reached for the leash, which she wordlessly handed over to him. "Honey?"

She blinked—twice.

"Is she on the run, too?" he asked impatiently, his gaze sliding in the direction the other dog had run off in.

"No," she said, slightly winded from her run through the orchards. "I put her in the house when Grits escaped his leash."

"He's not a fan of the leash," he told her. "I usually just let him out to run around with Honey in the yard to get their energy out."

"And they don't run away from you?" she asked in surprise.

Unlike you? he wanted to say. "No," he replied and then started into the orchard. "Grits and I will meet you back at Mrs. Tully's," he called back over his shoulder.

Lila has a son. That was all Mason could focus on as he went after the runaway pup. He shouldn't be surprised by the revelation. Not that she had made any mention of Finn when they'd spoken that first evening. But it had been nearly a decade since he'd last seen Lila. So much could change—apparently *had* changed—since then.

He cut through another row of peach trees, ducking to dodge a low-hanging branch. "Grits!" he called out, his gaze sweeping the area.

A distant bark had him shifting direction. Why did Grits have to get a burr in his fur britches, making him want to run that day of all days? But then, if he hadn't, Mason might never have discovered Lila had a son. Was Finn her only child? Or did she have a whole slew of them tucked away in the house? He shook his head. Lila having one child was more than enough to wrap his head around. He prayed Finn was the only surprise he would have during her stay there. He supposed he should prepare himself for the possibility of a husband showing up, as well.

Lord, please give me the strength to set my feelings, feelings I no longer have any right to, aside, and be the man my momma and daddy raised me to be. Thoughts of his father had him in turn wondering about Finn's. Who was the man who had succeeded where he had not in winning Lila's heart? The man who had the family Mason had once dreamed of. Once again, he found himself wondering why Mrs. Tully had kept so much from him—Lila's whereabouts, her marriage, her son. Had his neighbor, a woman both he and his family were quite fond of, done so in an effort to protect his feelings?

The sound of scampering feet in the not-too-far distance drew Mason from his troubled thoughts. Stopping, he cupped his hands to his mouth, calling out, "Grits! Here, boy!"

The dog appeared a few seconds later, bounding toward him with a peach held firmly in his mouth.

"There you are," he said with as much of

a smile as he could muster at that particular moment when he felt like doing anything but.

The pup stopped a few feet away and dropped the pilfered piece of fruit onto the ground, wagging his nubbin of a tail.

"I hate to break it to you, boy," he said as he calmly moved closer, "but that's a peach. Not a ball. What do you say we go back to the house and get you the real thing?" The pup glanced about as if contemplating another playful run, but Mason had reached him at this point and was able to grab ahold of his collar, then clipped on the leash. "Come on. Let's go get your red ball and get some of that extra energy out of you."

He let the pup lead the way. Grits knew his way home. He was one of the smartest dogs Mason had ever had the pleasure of knowing. A bit on the rambunctious side, but completely focused, with sharp reflexes.

When they reached his Gator, Mason settled Grits onto the passenger seat, making sure to hold on to his collar so he wouldn't jump out and injure himself.

The emotional snarl deep in his gut that he'd felt when Lila burst through the trees in search of Grits and the boy blossomed once again in his gut the moment he drove up to Mrs. Tully's place. Lila and Finn, who, judging by his size, looked to be around seven or so, waited for him on the front porch steps.

"Grits!" the young boy cried out. Shooting to his feet, he ran out to greet them.

"Back home safe and sound," Mason said, his gaze settling on Lila, who had pushed to her feet as well but remained where she was. "Why don't you take Grits in and give him some water?" he told her son, holding out the looped end of the leash. "Then find his ball and bring him back out. I'll run him a bit more before I trim the hedges."

"Okay," the boy said. A second later, both he and the dog were racing toward the house.

Mason knew he should have gone about his business there, but his feet had other plans, carrying him toward Lila. "I was on my way over here when I ran into your son and Grits." Not literally, thank the Lord. The whole scenario could have turned out far differently if either dog or boy had shot out from the trees a few second later. That thought in mind, he sent a quick prayer of thanks heavenward to the Lord for watching over Lila's son and Grits that day.

"I thought we had an agreement," Lila said with an accusatory glance.

"We do," he said, unsure of where she was going with this.

"You agreed to stop by between three and four o'clock on the days you need to tend to any yardwork."

His brows drew together in confusion at that remark. "Which is exactly what I've been doing," he replied.

"Then why were you on your way over here an hour early?" she asked.

"I wasn't."

"Oh," she said, some of the anger going out of her sails. "I thought you were headed to the house because of the direction you'd been heading when Finn came across you."

"I was," he said. "Just as we'd agreed upon. Timed it perfect, it seems, or you and *your son* might still be chasing Grits around the orchard."

"We would have managed," she told him, jutting her chin ever so slightly. "As for your having perfect timing, not even close." She held up her phone, showing him the time. "You're early."

Mason lifted his gaze back up to Lila's frowning face. "My apologies. I didn't realize you were referring to Central Daylight Time when you set the time I was allowed to stop by."

"What?" She turned the screen back to her and then lifted her gaze to Mason. "It's not 2:34 p.m. right now?"

"In the next time zone over," he replied. "Not here."

"Oh," she said, the rigidity leaving her posture. "I'm sorry. I don't know why my phone hasn't changed over to the correct time."

"Probably a setting in the phone," he surmised.

She nodded, her gaze falling away. "I'll look into it."

When she said nothing more, he said, "Why didn't you tell me?"

"Tell you what?" Her refusal to look him in the eye told him that Lila knew exactly what— no, make that *who*—he was referring to.

His frown deepened. "That you have a son," he said, doing his best to stuff down the jealousy. He didn't want to care that he wasn't a part of the cozy little picture that was Lila's life. Didn't want proof that Lila had found happiness without him. "Did you think that it would make any difference to me?" he asked, trying to keep his voice even.

She lifted her gaze, unshed tears looming in her eyes. "Mason—"

A bark cut into the words she'd been about to speak, drawing their attention to the porch, where both dogs darted out the door past Lila's son, leashes dragging behind them.

Finn scrambled down the porch steps

behind them, a colorful ball in each hand. "Stop!" he cried out as they raced off across the yard toward the trees.

"Oh no!" Lila gasped. "Not again."

Mason gave a sharp whistle, and both dogs stopped immediately and turned to face him. "Stay!" He crossed the yard, removed their leashes and then walked back to where Lila and her son stood watching.

"How did you do that?" Lila said in disbelief.

"We've been doing it every day since Mrs. Tully was admitted to the hospital," he told her. "Longer, actually. After she first took them in, I started coming by a couple of times a week to run some of their energy out for her."

"You always did have a thing for animals," she said with a soft smile.

Honey barked impatiently, causing Grits to follow suit.

Mason looked to Lila's son. "They're ready to play," he told him. "Give those balls a toss to the other side of the yard."

Finn did as instructed, sending them hurtling a fair distance across the yard.

"Good arm," Mason said with an acknowledging nod as the dogs raced after them. "A real ballplayer in the making. Your daddy must be proud." He knew he would be.

"I don't have one," the boy replied, the

smile that had been on his face as he'd watched the dogs retrieve the balls fading.

Mason stood there, dumbfounded by the boy's unexpected response. Then he looked to Lila.

"It's getting late," she said, looking past Mason to her son. "Honey and Grits appear to be in capable hands, and we need to get to the hospital. Gramma Tully is expecting us."

"Lila…" he said apologetically.

She finally turned to gaze his way. "That is, if you don't mind seeing to them this afternoon."

He shook his head. "No, not at all."

"Thank you," she said, her smile, like that of her son, all but gone. She started for the house, calling back over her shoulder for Finn.

The boy looked longingly at the dogs and then up at Mason, and then he was gone, hurrying after his mother.

Mason stood watching them go, his heart going out to Finn. He couldn't imagine growing up without a father. His daddy had been such an important part of his life. Along with teaching him the word of the Lord, he'd taught Mason how to ride a bike, play ball and work the orchard. Had Finn's died? Or had Lila and he divorced? Had Lila finally found her true happiness, only to lose it?

Chapter Three

Lila stood at the kitchen window, looking out at the extension of the Landerses' orchard their neighbors had added along the edge of Mama Tully's backyard. Of their own accord, her eyes searched among the rows of young peach trees for some sign of Mason. Her emotions warred, fearful of seeing him again now that he'd discovered she had a son, yet longing to see him.

Her hand moved to rest against her stomach, which had been tied up in knots all morning. She'd woken up knowing she needed to prepare herself for the confrontation that was certain to come. Mason might have been unaware of the enormity of the moment he'd first laid eyes on Finn, but it would come to him. It was just a matter of time before he figured it out. Once Mason replayed the events of the day before in his mind, finally processed what he'd seen, he would be back. Other than the wayward curls and smaller stature, which their son had inherited from her, Finn was the spitting image of his father. Maybe not so much the present-day Mason with his broad shoulders, deep voice and whisker-stubbled chin, but definitely of the younger version of the boy she had once loved.

Still loved, her foolish heart corrected. But how could she love a man she didn't know? Because the Mason she'd come home to was a stranger to her. They were no longer love-struck teens dreaming of a future together that would never come to fruition. They were adults with separate lives.

Barking erupted from somewhere at the front of the house, followed by scrambling footsteps and the shuffling of paws on the hardwood floors. A second later her son called out, "Mom! Mr. Landers is here."

Lila froze in place.

Heavy footsteps drew closer and stopped. Heart pounding, Lila turned. Mason stood unmoving, his gaze locked with hers. He was dressed in a pair of faded blue jeans and a navy blue T-shirt that hugged work-hewn arms, physical proof of the labor he put into his family's orchard. His jaw was set hard, his eyes accusing. And she knew without a doubt that this was it.

"Mason..." she began.

"We need to talk," he said in a gravelly tone, as if he were struggling to keep his emotions in check.

She nodded and then looked to her son, who, along with Grits and Honey, had followed Mason to the kitchen. *Their* son. "Sweetie, would you mind giving the dogs some fresh water and maybe a treat or two while Mr. Landers and I go discuss a few things?"

"Sure," he responded with a bright smile. Mason's smile.

Lila stepped away from the kitchen window and moved past Mason's imposing form, her heart pounding. He fell into step behind her. Thankfully, he waited until they were outside and well out of Finn's hearing to confront her.

"How old is he?" Mason demanded the moment they came to a stop next to Mama Tully's vegetable garden at the side of the house.

She knew Mason was referring to *their* son. But what if he threatened to take Finn away from her? Or what if he refused to acknowledge the child they'd conceived out of love was his? Any rejection of the child they had created together would break her heart. Gaze dropping to the ground between them, she answered, "Eight."

"Eight," he breathed as if trying to process the information.

"And a half," she added, feeling the sting of unshed tears.

A shocked gasp passed through Mason's lips. "Lila," he implored, his voice cracking with emotion, "is Finn my son?"

Lila forced herself to look up into Mason's accusing eyes. She'd expected anger, knew she was deserving of it no matter her reasons for doing what she'd done, but the hurt she saw there nearly had her sinking to her knees. "Yes," she said with a soft sob, hot tears spilling out onto her cheeks, "Finn is yours."

Moisture flooded his dark eyes as he stared down at her in disbelief. "I have a son."

She nodded with a sniffle. "You do. Mason…" she said, fear and regret threatening to swallow her up, "Finn doesn't know you're his father."

"I think that's pretty clear," he muttered with a frown. Dragging in a deep, steadying breath, he ran a hand down over his face and then pinned her with an accusatory gaze. "Why would you keep him from me? I loved you. I thought you loved me."

"I do," she countered with a hiccupping sob. "I... I mean, I did."

"You have, or should I say *had*," he amended, "a funny way of expressing your love for me. Taking off without a word, unless you count that brief goodbye letter you left behind for me. And then there's the child you were carrying when you ran off, *my* son, who you chose to keep from me for more than eight years."

"I left because I loved you," she insisted. "If I had stayed in Sweet Springs, it would have caused you and your family shame. Caused Mama Tully shame. And it would have meant an end to your dream of following in your daddy's footsteps, something I truly believed you wanted to do at the time."

He glanced off toward the house where their son was, thankfully oblivious to the torrent of emotions whirling about outside. Then he turned back to Lila. "You should have talked to me. Should have trusted me."

There was no denying the hurt she heard in his voice. More hurt than anger at that moment, which only deepened her guilt. Before Lila could respond, a melodic tune started playing in the back pocket of her jeans. The hospital and Addy were the only ones who would be calling her, but they would have to wait. Right now, she needed to focus on Mason and what he intended to do now that he knew the truth.

Mason frowned as the ringtone continued to drift up between them. "You'd best answer that. It might be the hospital."

Reluctantly, she slipped the phone free of her pocket and had to squint to read the display on the screen beneath the bright glare of the afternoon sun. Even then, the words were blurred thanks to her tear-filled eyes. A second later, Lila looked up at him as she answered the call. "It's the hospital." Bringing the phone to her ear, she said, "Hello?"

There was a long pause and then Mason saw Lila's worried expression deepen. "And how long will that take?" she asked the caller on the other end, her voice cracking with emotion.

Without thinking, he started to move closer to offer her his support, but then caught himself and pulled back. What kind of fool would try to offer emotional support to the woman who kept his child from him for eight years?

"I see," she said in response to whatever had been said on the other end of the line. "Yes. Please let her know I'll be there as soon

as possible. Thank you for contacting me."
Ending the call, she lifted her gaze to his.

"Something wrong?" he queried, despite
already knowing the answer. The hospital
wouldn't call an emergency contact to exchange idle chatter.

"Yes," Lila replied, tears pooling thick
in her eyes. "She's developed a slight fever.
They're running tests—blood work, I think
the doctor said—to see what's causing it and
what kind of antibiotic is needed to treat it.
What if the peritonitis has come back? Or
worse," she said, swaying slightly as if her
legs might give way beneath her at any moment, "what if it's turned to sepsis?"

Despite his feelings of betrayal, Mason
moved to wrap a supportive arm about her
shoulders. "*Slight* fever, Lila," he stressed.
"That means they've caught whatever it is
early and can get her the proper medication
to clear up any infection."

She nodded, sending another tear down her
already dampened cheek.

He unthinkingly reached up to swipe it
away with his thumb, a gesture that felt so
natural when it should be anything but. Letting his hand fall back to his side, Mason said,
"She's going to be okay."

"I can't lose her," she sobbed. "She and Addy are all we have."

Her words stabbed at his heart, a heart that was at that moment already feeling shredded to pieces. She would have had him, too, if she'd only stuck around to see things through, instead of running off with his child. "You won't lose her," he said assuredly, letting his arm fall away. Then he sent a prayer heavenward, asking the Lord to see Mrs. Tully safely through this new setback.

"I'm so sorry," she said with a sniffle. "I know there's so much more we need to talk about, but I have to go."

"Agreed," he acknowledged with a nod. "We'll discuss things later. You need to be with Mrs. Tully right now."

"Yes." Her hand shook as she slid her phone back into the pocket of her jeans.

"Get your things," he told her. "I'll take you and Finn to the hospital."

She looked more than a little surprised by his offer. He supposed he was, as well. She didn't deserve any favors from him, but she didn't need to be sitting behind the wheel of a car now with his son inside. *His son.* He'd never thought he'd be anyone's father. After Lila had run out on him, he'd locked those hopes and dreams up tight and focused on running and improving the orchards and family market.

"There's no need—" Lila began, but he cut her off.

"You're in no condition to drive," he pointed out. "Besides, *I* need to know Mrs. Tully is all right."

"I would never do anything to hurt my son," she said defensively.

He raised a challenging brow, tempted to point out that she had intentionally kept Finn from knowing who his father was. But there would be time enough for addressing the choices she had made. "*Our* son," he clarified.

Lowering her gaze, she nodded.

"I'll go put Honey and Grits in their room," Mason said with a sigh of frustration. "You and Finn gather up whatever you need and meet me out at my truck." He started for the house.

Hurried footsteps sounded behind him as Lila hurried to catch up. "Mason…"

He glanced her way.

"Please, I beg you," she said, "let me be the one to tell Finn the truth."

He didn't owe Lila anything. But he did owe his son the chance to hear the truth from someone the boy trusted and loved, not from the father he'd never known. Stopping, he turned to face her. "You have a week to tell our son what he should have known all along," he allowed. "If you haven't done so by then, I will."

"I'll tell him," she said shakily.

With a nod, he walked away, replaying that day in the orchard in his mind. How had he not seen the truth from the first moment he saw Finn? The same dark shade of hair as his own. And those eyes…he thought with a mental headshake. Like his, they were a deep, dark brown. Finn's face was the same face that had stared back at him in the bathroom mirror when he was a boy. Mason's lungs constricted as the enormity of it all sank in. He had a son.

Once they'd arrived at the hospital, Mason, Lila and their son—how odd to think of another human being as a part of him—made their way down the long entryway corridor. Finn, who had begun dragging his feet the moment they had stepped out of Mason's truck, came to a sudden stop next to an alcove housing a pair of vending machines. "Momma…"

Mason, who had taken up the rear, nearly walked right over him. It was only his reflexive grasp hooking onto his son's narrow shoulders that kept him from stumbling forward.

Thankful he hadn't plowed his son over, Mason released his hold on Finn's shoulder and looked to Lila. "I didn't expect him to stop short."

She started back toward them. "Finn?" Her worried gaze zeroed in on the little boy. "Honey, why did you stop?"

"I'm thirsty," he told her, looking to the nearby vending machines. "And hungry."

"We don't have time to stop right now," she explained with a motherly smile. "We need to look in on Gramma Tully first."

"Momma," their son pleaded, "I don't want to see Gramma Tully sick."

Gramma Tully? Mason supposed he shouldn't be surprised to hear Finn refer to Mrs. Tully as such. But family, whether blood related or not, was so important. He hadn't truly appreciated that until Lila had come into his life. A young girl with no one to turn to, to guide her, to love her. Mrs. Tully had given her those things and so much more.

His attention went back to Lila, who had reached out to lightly stroke Finn's dark curls. Her curls, only looser. Their son was an undeniable mix of the two of them. "Oh, sweetie, it's just a teeny, tiny fever. Nothing to worry yourself over."

Mason looked to his son and offered him a reassuring smile. "Why don't you go have a look at what's available in those machines while your momma and I have a few words?"

Finn looked to his mother, who nodded her consent, and then happily took the detour he'd been hoping for.

"I suppose a hospital isn't the most comfortable environment for a young boy," Mason said, keeping his voice low, despite Finn having already disappeared into the small snack room.

"No," she said, shaking her head in agreement. "He's not a fan. But he's done so well since his first visit here, when he was a bit overwhelmed by all the sounds and various hospital equipment. I thought he was past his fear of this place."

"Tell you what," Mason said. "Why don't you go on ahead and look in on Mrs. Tully? I'll stay back with Finn and grab a couple bottles of water and some snacks for all of us. We don't know how long it'll be before we'll be able to go have lunch."

"True," she agreed, yet she appeared to be torn about leaving him alone with their son.

"If you're worried about me telling Finn the

truth, you never really knew me," he said in frustration. "I gave you my word back at the house, and I have no intention of breaking it. No matter how that is going to be."

"I do know you," she replied softly. "Or did. And my heart tells me you haven't changed."

No, it was Lila who couldn't be trusted. "I thought this might give him a little time to get into a better mind-set before he sees Mrs. Tully. And it would also keep him from seeing her if she's not faring well."

"I should have considered that."

"You have other things on your mind," he told her. Like the lie she'd been living for the past nine years. But it wasn't the time or place to get into her unforgivable actions. "Finn and I will meet you at Mrs. Tully's room in a little while. If she's not up to our company, give me a call and we'll wait for you here."

She glanced into the alcove with a frown. "That's probably a good idea."

"We both want what's best for *our* son," he said quietly. And it was true. Neither of them knew what they would find once they got to Mrs. Tully's room.

Before Lila could respond, Finn stepped out of the alcove to join them.

"See anything you like?" Mason asked, glancing his way.

His son gave a slight shrug. "Some stuff."

"Give me one sec to give your momma my cell number in case she needs to reach us, and then you can show me what you found. She's going to go on ahead to check on your gramma Tully. You and I will meet her after we pick out a few snacks to bring to the room with us."

"*Healthy* snacks," Lila inserted as she handed Mason her phone to put his number into.

"Would I choose any other kind?" Mason asked as he typed his number in.

"I remember all too well what you tried to pass off as being healthy when we were growing up."

"I promise not to be swayed by the not-so-nutritious choices," he assured her as he handed her back her cell phone.

"Fine," she said, and then looked down at her son. "Be sure to mind your manners."

"I will, Momma."

As Lila hurried away, Mason accompanied his son back into the snack alcove.

"Okay, so what's caught your eye?" Mason asked and then added with a grin, "Keep in mind that I promised your mom we'd make choices that will help keep you healthy and strong."

Finn stood staring at the selections in front of him in silence.

"Everything okay?" Mason asked.

His son shrugged.

"Are you worried about your gramma Tully?"

Finn gave a slow nod. "I don't like her being sick."

He offered his son a consoling smile. "None of us do. That's why we trust in the doctors to see to her care, while we do our part by taking the time to pray for her."

"I don't know how," his son admitted, looking up at Mason with tears pooling in his dark eyes. "Is that why Gramma's getting sick again? Because I didn't pray for her?"

The statement made Mason feel like he'd been knocked backward. Surely he had misunderstood. Was it possible that Lila had not taught Finn how to pray? That would change. He'd see to it personally. Reaching out to place a comforting hand on his son's slender shoulder, he said, "Nothing about her illness is your fault. Sometimes, during the healing process, people take a few steps forward followed by an occasional baby step backward. This just happens to be one of those pesky baby steps. Your gramma Tully will weather it. We just have to have faith."

"Can I have faith if I don't know how to pray?" his son asked.

"They kind of go hand in hand," Mason

explained. "How about you and I say a quick prayer for her together?"

Finn nodded, his worried frown easing. "If it'll make Gramma Tully better."

"A little bit of praying never hurts," Mason told him. "Let's take a moment to bow our heads. I'll guide you through the rest."

"Where's the fire?" Mama Tully asked as Lila rushed into her hospital room.

Lila crossed the room to the bed and reached for the older woman's hand. "The hospital called and said you had developed a fever and they were running tests." Now that she had a moment to look Mama Tully over, Lila had to admit she didn't look too feverish. At least not as bad as she had imagined when she'd gotten the call from the on-duty nurse.

Mama Tully waved a hand of dismissal. "People make such a fuss over a slight rise in my temperature. I feel fine." She looked past Lila expectantly. "Where's Finn?"

"He was hungry. Mason offered to wait with him in the snack area while you and I visited for a bit," she answered automatically, as if her son being with Mason Landers was the most normal thing in the world. It wasn't. And now that she thought about, her anxiety deepened…

"Mason is with Finn?" Mama Tully asked in surprise, drawing Lila from her troubled thoughts.

"Yes."

The older woman's face lit up. But then it could simply be her fever making it appear so. "Does that mean he knows?"

"That you're a bit under the weather today?" Lila surmised and then nodded. "Yes, I told Finn before we left for the hospital. I wanted him to be prepared in case things had gotten worse by the time we got here. Which is why he was a bit reluctant to come to your room. But he needed to know the truth. Mason was at the house when the call came and insisted on driving us to the hospital."

"I wasn't referring to Finn," Mama Tully said. "I was referring to Mason."

"What about Mason?"

"Have you told him the truth?"

Lila's stomach dropped. "The truth?"

"About his being Finn's father," Mama Tully said without reservation.

Here it is, she thought to herself, heart pounding. The truth that had been unspoken between them for the two years Lila and she had been in contact again. Legs trembling beneath her, Lila sank down into the chair beside the bed. "You knew," she said, more a statement than a question.

"I'd had my wonderings. Especially when you did everything you could to avoid discussing who Finn's daddy was. I realize there was a possibility there could have been someone else in your life after you ran off, but I couldn't see that happening. You were too in love with Mason when you lived in Sweet Springs. But the first moment I laid eyes on Finn in my hospital room I knew for certain. Your son looks just like the little boy who grew up next door to me. Granted, he's a bit smaller in stature than Mason was at that age, but then you've always been a wisp of a thing. And that's why you never wanted to come back here, isn't it?"

Lila lowered her gaze, shame and embarrassment filling her. She had kept the truth from so many people she loved. And to have done that to Mama Tully felt like such a betrayal of all that trust and love. "Yes," she said softly.

"You know, honey, nearly dying made me realize how important it is to never leave things that need saying unsaid," Mama Tully said reflectively. "Mason deserves to know the truth."

"He already does," Lila said reluctantly.

"And Finn?"

"We haven't told him yet," she replied. "Mason only just found out today, right before we left for the hospital."

"I see. And how did he take the news?"

"Not well, but I can't blame him for feeling the way he does." She frowned. "He's given me a week to tell Finn the truth. If I haven't, he's made it clear that he's going to tell Finn himself."

"Honey, I have to say that's more than generous of him, all things considered," Mama Tully said.

"I know," Lila agreed with a soft sob. Not only had she kept Finn from his daddy, but she'd also kept him from having his gramma Tully for all those lost years. A woman who would have showered Finn with love, just as she once had Lila.

"Oh, Lila, sweetie, I can see how heavily this is weighing on you," her foster mother said consolingly, despite the disappointment Lila could see in the older woman's eyes.

"It is," Lila admitted. "It has for years."

"What I don't understand is why you didn't tell Mason the truth when you first learned you were expecting," Mama Tully said, her expression troubled. "That young man used to wear his heart on his sleeve where you were concerned, and I thought you felt the same way about him."

"I did."

"But you left him with barely a word of explanation," she pointed out, her tone gentle. "I've not brought up the past during our phone conversations because I was afraid of pushing you away. But I'm asking you now. Why didn't you come to me or someone else, especially Mason? Lord knows things might have been a bit complicated for the two of you at first, but you would have found a way to make things work with mine and his family's love and support."

Complicated, Lila thought, her heart aching. Exactly what Mason preferred to avoid. "I left because I loved Mason," Lila said in a choked sob, guilt and regret filling her. "We were both so young, and he had his heart set on following in his daddy's footsteps."

"He didn't, though."

"I know that now," Lila said sullenly. "But I was so worried about hurting everyone that I didn't allow myself to consider the what-ifs. I knew shame. Lived with it most of my childhood, having had parents who were constantly intoxicated or on drugs, sometimes both."

"Oh, sweetie," Mama Tully groaned with an empathetic frown.

"I wanted to protect Mason and his family, and you. Our being so young, not to mention unwed, while expecting a child would have made his becoming a respected man of the cloth an incredibly difficult path to travel down. It would have undoubtedly brought shame to his family, and they had always been so welcoming to me. And it would have hurt you," she said, tearing up. Not to mention Mason would have felt obligated to marry her. That would have left her questioning if that was what he'd truly wanted, though they had talked about doing just that. What if he'd gone off to school and met someone else, or simply realized the dreams they'd shared were no longer the ones he wanted?

"That was a hurt I could have gotten over," Mama Tully told her. "A far lesser hurt than what I lived through."

"I'm so sorry," Lila said, the reminder of the pain she'd cause her beloved foster mother causing her apology to catch in her throat. "You were the closest thing to a mother I've ever had. I couldn't bear the thought of my actions reflecting badly on you or causing you to hate me."

Now Mama Tully's eyes were tearing up. "I could never hate you, Lila. I just wish you had come to me. We could have figured things out together. It hurt me deeply when you ran away, but now, knowing what I do, I can understand how very scary an unplanned pregnancy must have been for you. Especially given the life you lived before coming to Sweet Springs."

"Getting pregnant at seventeen, even if Mason and I had only ever been together in that way one time, was a sin I've had to live with for the past nine years," Lila said, pain tearing at her heart. Not that she could ever regret the sweet blessing she'd been given. "A sin that has kept me away from the faith you brought into my life."

"The Lord is good, Lila," Mama Tully told her. "Ask for His forgiveness and accept it as so in your heart."

She gave a slow nod. She would try. And while God might forgive her, she knew Mason never would. Lila hung her head. "I'm so sorry I hurt you."

"No," her foster mother said, "I'm the one who's sorry. Sorry you didn't feel secure enough to trust me with the truth. Sorry I didn't let you know how much you meant to me. You were the daughter I had always prayed for but couldn't make my own because of the system and its sometimes complicated rules. After your parents passed away, I made up my mind to look into adopting you."

Lila's head lifted instantly, her tear-dampened eyes wide. "You did?" she gasped in disbelief.

"I did," she said tenderly. "Even though I knew you would be legally an adult by the time we made it to court, I was determined to see if it was possible."

"You never said anything," Lila said, reaching for the older woman's hand, which rested atop the white hospital sheet. Would that have made a difference if she had known? She wished she could say it would have, because it meant the world to her, but she still would have left.

"I didn't want to get your hopes up in case it was all for naught. But my prayers were answered. I learned that an adoption could take place despite your being of legal age and planned to tell you on your eighteenth birthday."

Lila sat, still trying to process what she had just learned. Mama Tully had wanted to adopt her. "Thank you for loving me enough to have wanted to make me yours. Having you as a mother would have been one of the biggest blessings the Lord could have bestowed upon me."

"Thank you for saying that," Mama Tully

said with a warm smile. "I will always be your mother. Maybe not by blood, but in my heart."

Lila was beyond touched.

"And speaking of blessings," Mama Tully went on, "the biggest one of all is right down that hall out there with the father he has always deserved. You and Mason need to set aside the past now and work things out for the sake of your son."

"If only it were that simple," Lila countered. It was complicated. Oh, there was that word again. It was as if it had taken a stranglehold on her life and on her heart.

"Life rarely is," Mama Tully replied with a nod. "But, sweetie, you have to know Mason's been given a lot to deal with. He's going to need time. Things are going to change for all of you. It's inevitable. The most important thing is that you make those changes positive for Finn. You of all people understand how having, or not having, a parent or parents in one's life can affect a child."

She did, because she'd not only missed out on having her father in her life, but her mother, as well. Mason hadn't been given a choice, but her heart told her he would have chosen to have Finn be a part of his life, no matter the consequences. Guilt for the choices she had made ate at her.

"I'm not sure where Mason's thoughts are regarding Finn," Lila told her. "He had just found out the truth about Finn when the hospital called. But he'd already made it clear when we first ran into each other that anything we once shared is in the past," she said, her heart hurting at the truth of it. "And that he doesn't need or want any complications in his life."

"But Finn isn't—"

"A complication?" Lila finished for her. "Can you tell me that finding out he has a son isn't going to affect Mason's entire life now? Or wouldn't have done nine years ago?"

Mama Tully frowned. "Of course it will. But that boy is a blessing, no matter the circumstances of his arrival into this world."

"I'm afraid Mason will decide that it's more than he's ready to take on. I don't want to see my son hurt."

"I think you know Mason better than that," Mama Tully scolded lightly. "His heart is every bit as caring and loving as it was when the two of you were together. He will love your son, his son, with everything he has in him."

"While I know things will never be the way they once were between us, I hope I can rebuild even a piece of the friendship Mason and I once had for Finn's sake. In the meantime, I need to figure out the gentlest way to tell my son the truth about his father."

"The sooner the better," her foster mother said. "He deserves to have as much time as possible bonding with his son before he has to leave."

"Leave?" Lila repeated.

"Mason is heading to the Congo soon to do some missionary work."

Lila gasped, "Why would Mason go there?"

"Should my ears be burning?"

Lila spun around as Mason and Finn entered the room.

He held a bottle of vitamin-infused water out to her. "Finn tells me you have a thing for flavored waters."

"I do." She took the bottle with a grateful smile.

"I hope we're not interrupting anything," he said, glancing between her and Mama Tully. "Finn was ready to see his gramma Tully."

"I brought you chocolate," her son said with a smile as he walked over to deliver it to his gramma Tully.

Mama Tully's smile spread across her face as she accepted the gift. "My favorite," she said happily, wasting no time in peeling away the wrapper. She looked to Mason. "I was just telling Lila about your upcoming mission trip."

"Why the Congo?" Lila asked worriedly as she stood looking up into his handsome face.

"Because those children deserve the chance to have an education and to learn about the word of God," he answered without even a moment's hesitation. "I'm going to help with the building of a new school over there."

"I wish you would reconsider," she said, as if she had any right to even suggest such a thing. But what if Mason went over there and never came back for some reason? Finn would have learned he had a father, only to lose him.

He looked to Finn. "I wish I could, but the paperwork is already in motion, and people are counting on my help."

But you have a son now, she wanted to say. Lila looked to Finn and then back to Mason. "When will you be leaving?"

"End of summer. Once the harvesting is done."

Far too soon. Lila found herself doing something she'd rarely done since leaving Sweet Springs—praying, because she'd realized her son deserved to have his father in his life. Even though she'd kept Mason from Finn all these years.

Chapter Four

"Can I get you anything else?" Lila asked as she straightened the additional blanket she had just spread out across the top of Mama Tully's bedspread. Her foster mother had been released a few days before from the hospital. Although still weak from the ordeal, she was infection free. Other than needing to finish the entire bottle of antibiotics they sent home with her and a follow up visit with her physician, Mama Tully was well on the mend. "A glass of water or cup of hot tea?"

"I'm fine. Thank you," the older woman answered with a grateful smile. "I just need to catch up on my sleep. They don't believe in letting you rest through the night at the hospital. Always wanting to poke and prod me. But I wouldn't be lying here in my own bed, in my own house, if it weren't for the grace of God and the dedication of the doctors and nurses who took care of me during my stay there."

Lila nodded. As she moved toward the door, Mama Tully called out to her.

"You do remember what tomorrow is, don't you?"

Stopping in the doorway, she turned to look at her foster mother. "Thursday?"

Mama Tully shook her head. "I'm not referring to the day of the week. I'm referring to the deadline Mason gave you. You only have until tomorrow to talk to Finn."

"I haven't forgotten." Although Mason had made himself scarce in the past week, the few glimpses she'd had of him had been enough to stir up her whirling emotions all the more.

"Honey, I know you're afraid," Mama Tully said tenderly. "But everything is going to work out just fine. You'll see."

Going over and over the right words to tell Finn this past week in her head was emotionally taxing. No matter how she pieced her explanation together, there was no denying that the choice she had made all those years ago had been wrong. She saw that now. Lila leaned her head against the door frame with a sigh. "Finn's been so happy here, looking after Honey and Grits, spending time with you after waiting so long to finally meet you in person."

Mama Tully's smile warmed all the more. "I've enjoyed spending time with him, too. That smile of his just melts my heart."

"Mine, too." Lila nodded. "He's always been a happy, carefree child, but here his joy is constantly written on his face. That's why I dread the thought of turning my son's world upside down and taking that joy away. Because finally learning the truth is going to do just that."

"Have you ever considered that finally knowing the truth might actually turn Finn's world right side up?" Mama Tully countered. "Not only will he finally have a daddy, he'll have an extended family who will love the stuffing right out of him."

"What if they can't open their hearts to him?" Lila asked with a troubled frown.

"It's Finn," Mama Tully replied. "It's impossible not to love that boy."

The words touched Lila's heart, and she nodded in agreement. With a soft sniffle, she said, "Mama Tully, I've really missed having you in my life to talk things over with." They'd had several heart-to-hearts since her foster mother came home from the hospital, spending treasured hours reconnecting.

Their discussions hadn't all been sunshine and flowers. They'd discussed Mama Tully's fears for the young girl who'd taken off into what could be a big, scary world and Lila's fears for the child she had brought into the world alone. Thankfully, Addy had been there for her. But the fear of letting her child down, as her own parents had her, remained a constant in her mind. That was the biggest reason, if she were being honest with herself, for her putting off her talk with Finn. What she had to tell him would inevitably shake the trust her son had in her. But he needed to know the truth. Deserved to know it. She just needed to make him understand her reasons.

"Having you and Finn here has done my heart good," Mama Tully told her, tears filling her eyes, as well. "Now I just need to get my other girl home and all my prayers will be answered."

"Addy's anxious to see you, too." Lila cast a glance back over her shoulder. "I should go check on Finn and the pups and let you get to sleep." Looking back to Mama Tully, she said, "Thank you for being so supportive."

Mama Tully smiled tiredly. "That's what mommas do."

Not all of them, Lila thought, recalling her own birth mother. Thankfully, Mama Tully had come into her life. Even now, after all the hurt Lila had caused her by leaving the way she had, Mama Tully still loved her. Heart in her throat, Lila said, "Sleep well." Stepping from the room, she eased the door shut behind her and then went in search of her son.

Lila found her son sitting on the porch, playing with Honey and Grits. She'd constructed a barricade for the steps using some old wood planks she'd found in the back shed and chicken coop fencing. The makeshift blockade could be easily slid to the side, giving access to the steps. It was enough of a deterrent to keep the rambunctious dogs from running off when they weren't on their leashes. Mason might have easy command of the pups, but Lila had not mastered that particular ability yet.

Finn glanced up, the overhead porch light casting a soft glow over her son's toothy grin as he looked up at her. "Where's Gramma Tully?"

Mama Tully had spent the past couple of evenings sitting out on the front porch with them, tucked comfortably beneath a lap quilt in her favorite white wicker rocker.

"She's still needing to catch up on her sleep, so she decided to turn in early tonight,"

Lila told him as she settled cross-legged on the porch floor next to him.

"I'm glad she's home," he said, his focus returning to Grits, who had just dropped his ball onto Finn's lap. The energetic dog promptly backed up several steps and then waited, tail wagging, for him to throw it.

"Me, too," Lila agreed.

Reaching out to Honey, who was stretched out lazily a couple feet away, Lila stroked the contented pup behind her ears.

"Do you think Mr. Landers will be by tomorrow?" her son asked distractedly.

Lila's hand stilled, a knot forming instantly in her stomach. Mason would be by. Of that she had no doubt.

"He hasn't been back since he took us to see Gramma Tully at the hospital when she got her fever," her son went on. Finn and Mason already shared an undeniable connection.

While Mason had done his best to avoid coming around like he had been, for reasons Finn couldn't understand, he still called Mama Tully every day to check on her and see if she needed anything.

The insecure young girl inside Lila feared his absence could be because he was having second thoughts about being Finn's father.

Lila mentally strong-armed that thought away. It was more likely he had avoided coming around because the temptation to tell Finn the truth would be far too great. Something Mason wouldn't do, his having given his word not to. At least, until the week he'd allotted her was up.

"Harvest season tends to take up a lot of time, and Mason plays a big part in the running of his family's orchard and business," Lila explained. "But I'm sure we'll see him soon." Grits came over and dropped his ball onto Lila's lap and then raced away. Grateful for the interruption, she picked up the ball and she tossed it to him. "Nice catch," she praised as Grits exaggeratedly leaped into the air and caught the arcing ball.

"He never misses," her son said in awe. "I wish I could catch as good as him."

"Maybe your da—" Lila caught herself just in time. She'd spent years avoiding any mention of Mason, but now that he finally knew the truth, all she could think about was that Finn would finally have a daddy. *A real ballplayer in the making. Your daddy must be proud.* Mason's praise for Finn that day her son was throwing the ball had been kind and encouraging.

Mama Tully's reminder that her week was

at an end tapped impatiently at the forefront of her mind. She was right. There was no more putting it off. "Finn, honey, how about we put the pups inside and take a short walk before turning in for the night?"

"In the dark?" he replied in surprise.

"There's a hint of moonlight peeking out through those clouds," she assured him. "And we won't go far."

"Can we walk through the orchard?" he asked excitedly.

Her gaze moved in that direction. How fitting it would be, that she would she tell her son the truth about his father among the fruit trees that meant so much to Mason and his family. Nodding, she got to her feet and called the dogs, luring them inside with the promise of a treat. "Be right back," she told Finn as she followed Honey and Grits into the house.

A few minutes later, she returned, heart in her throat. "Ready?" she asked her son with a forced smile.

"Yep," he answered. Reaching out, he slid the makeshift fence aside and bounded excitedly down the steps.

Lila followed, her steps feeling weighted.

"Come on, Momma!"

"I'm coming," she replied, picking up her step. Once again, the sweet aroma of ripening peaches stirred memories of her past, of what would assuredly be a part of her son's future. Would Mason demand shared custody? And how would that work, with her living in Alabama and Finn enrolled in school there? Then a more unsettling thought stirred. What if he sought full custody?

If she and God were in a better place, she would ask for guidance for what she was about to do. But her long-held guilt had opened a seemingly uncrossable chasm between herself and the religion Mama Tully and the Landers family had helped her to find as a young girl. As it stood, this was something she was going to have to do on her own.

"Finn…" she called out.

He stopped skipping along the moonlit, well-worn grass path and turned to look at her.

"I need to talk to you about something."

Not missing the seriousness in her tone, he asked solemnly, "Is Gramma Tully sick again?"

She shook her head as she closed the short distance between them. "No, not at all. She's getting better every day."

The moon's light danced off her son's face as clouds drifted across the night sky. He looked so very much like his father. "We're not going back to Alabama yet, are we? Is that what you want to talk about?"

Was that disappointment she heard in his voice? Was it possible Finn preferred life in Sweet Springs to the life she'd built for them elsewhere? If that were the case, would he choose to stay with his father?

"No," she told him. "Not until Addy can come look after Gramma Tully. I wanted to talk to you about something else. About you, actually."

"Me?"

"You've asked me before about your daddy."

His eyes widened.

"When I was a young girl, I was in love with a very special boy," she continued, before she could lose her nerve and put their talk off yet again.

"But he didn't love you?" her son surmised.

"I believe he loved me very much," she replied. "We both had hopes and dreams for our future. One we planned to spend together forever."

"Then why did he leave us?" Finn demanded, hurt in his voice.

Tears filled her eyes as the memories washed over her. "He didn't know there was an us. I never told him we were going to be having a baby—*you*."

"Why?"

"When you're as young as your daddy and I were, just stepping out into the real world of adulthood, you're not prepared for the changes a baby would bring. I wanted your daddy to have his dreams, even if I couldn't be a part of them, so I left Sweet Springs without telling him about you."

"What if he'd wanted me and not his dreams?" her son demanded, his voice gritty with emotion.

"I've no doubt he would have wanted you," she said, a lone tear sliding down her cheek. "But I was trying to do the right thing."

"By taking my daddy away?" he said.

She reached for him, but he pulled away. "Finn…"

"You said you loved my daddy, but you left him. Will you leave me, too?" he asked, both fear and anger lacing his voice.

"Never," she replied, aghast at the very thought of it. "You are my world."

"I should have been my daddy's world, too." His expression changed from one of anger to dawning realization. "You said you left Sweet Springs?"

"I did."

"Then my daddy lives here?"

She nodded. "He does, and you've met him."

His dark eyes widened. "I have?"

As if in response to the emotional turmoil, more clouds pushed in across the night sky, tamping out the moonlight and casting them in near total darkness.

"Yes," she said, her throat constricting.

"Who?" he demanded, his small, hurt voice carrying in the night.

"Mason," she replied, wanting desperately to gather her son in her arms and ease his hurt. "Mr. Landers is your daddy."

Tiny sobs rose up in the air around her, breaking Lila's heart. "Finn," she said, reaching toward his shadowy outline once more.

And once again he pulled away, shattering her. And then, without a word, he turned and ran off into the night.

"Finn!" she called after him. "Sweetie, please come back so we can talk."

But her son was gone. The rhythmic chirping of the katydids was the only sound to be heard. Pulling out her cell phone, Lila clicked on the flashlight and set off after her heartbroken child.

An urgent pounding at the front door drew Mason's attention from the dinner he'd been enjoying with his family. Jake, seated closest to the open doorway, shot up from his seat and hurried to answer it.

"Lila?" Mason heard his brother say in surprise.

"Is Mason here?" she blurted out in a panting sob. "Please, I need Mason."

Mason was up and on his feet, hurrying out into the entryway in long, urgent strides, before his brother had a chance to respond. "Lila," he called out.

"Mason," she said, her breathing labored. Twin streaks of dampness trailed down her cheeks. Tears clung to her thick lashes, readying to fall. "He's gone and I can't find him."

He's gone. He didn't have to ask to know that Lila was referring to Finn.

"Grits will come back," Jake said, his tone less than sympathetic. "He's probably just off chasing a rabbit. What I don't understand is your thinking Mason would have even the slightest inclination to help you after—"

"Jake," Mason snarled. "Stay out of this."

His brother looked at him in shock.

"What on earth is all the commotion..." His mother's words trailed off as her gaze landed on Lila.

Violet was right on their mother's heels, casting a disapproving scowl in Lila's direction the moment she saw her.

His family would have to wait for explanations. Right now he had to find out what had happened. Turning his focus back to Lila, he asked, "What happened? Where's Finn?"

She shook her head, more tears spilling out. "I don't know. We were taking a walk in the orchard and he ran off."

"In the dark?" he asked with a frown.

"The moon was out when we left," she told him. "I know I shouldn't have come here, but I didn't know what else to do. I've been searching for him for nearly an hour. I thought he might have come to you."

"Why would he come to—"

"Because he knows the truth," she told him.

The *truth*. That word made Mason's heart thud. Finn knew he was his father. Then panic set in. Not only because his son was out there somewhere in the dark all alone, but because he didn't exactly know what had sent Finn running.

"Mason," his momma said, "what's going on?"

He turned to his family, regretful that this was how they were going to find out, but his son was out there in the dark somewhere, scared, heart hurting. "Finn is Lila's son." He looked to Lila. "*Our* son."

"What?" his sister gasped.

"Honey?" his momma croaked out.

"You've never said anything about having a son," his little brother said, sounding both hurt and angry. As if Mason had intentionally betrayed his trust.

"He didn't know," Lila said in his defense.

"We'll explain everything after our son is found safe and sound," Mason told them. He supposed he should feel shame, but he had sought forgiveness for his and Lila's actions that day a long time ago. Now all he felt was awe at the thought of having a son, and, at that moment, worry, because Finn was out there, dealing with the shock, alone and in the dark. "Right now, we need to find Finn." On a night like this one, it would be easy to get turned around in the orchard. Even for someone who knew their way around.

"Yes," his brother said, moving toward the hall closet. "We do."

"I'm going, too," Violet said determinedly.

Their mother joined Jake at the closet. "Hand me the lantern. I'll go look around the market buildings."

Jake handed it back to her.

"I'll go with Momma," his sister volunteered.

Reaching into the storage closet, Jake retrieved several heavy-duty flashlights. "I'll take the Gator over and search the new orchard."

"Be careful," Mason warned. "We don't know where Finn is."

Nodding, Jake handed one of the flashlights over to Violet and one to Mason, keeping the remaining one for himself. Looking to Lila, he said, "Sorry, there aren't any extras."

"She won't need one," Mason told him. "She'll be with me." Taking Lila's hand in his, he led her off the porch and out into the night. Once they were away from the house, he released her hand and headed for the most northern section of the orchard.

"Finn!" he called out, his voice carrying in the night.

Silence greeted them.

"He's never done this before," Lila said brokenly as she hurried to keep up beside him. "What if he's hurt?"

There were all sorts of hazards out there in the orchard: a hole in the ground he could twist an ankle in or low-hanging branches that might catch Finn in the eye. "All we can do is pray to God to keep our son safe and have faith we'll find him soon."

Lila fell silent, drawing Mason's gaze in her direction.

"When did you stop praying, Lila?" he

asked the dark outline beside him, wishing he could see her face. "Because the girl I fell in love with welcomed the Lord into her life."

"The day I found out I was pregnant."

"It wasn't God's fault," he said with a frown.

"I know that. I don't blame Him," she explained. "I blame myself."

"And for that our son has suffered spiritually," he told her, as if she wasn't already aware of it. "And before you deny it, Finn told me so himself that day we rushed to the hospital to see Mrs. Tully."

"I wasn't going to."

"Finn!" Mason did another sweep of the grounds around them with the flashlight, still seeing no sign of his son. With a sigh, he moved onward.

They walked in silence except for when they called out for Finn. Mason's gut was churning with worry. So this was what it felt like to be a father. To worry about a life you'd created. A buzzing in his back pocket had him grabbing for his phone. "It's Jake," he told Lila as he answered. "Hello?"

"I've got him," his brother said, sending relief spiraling through Mason.

"Is he okay?" he asked anxiously.

"As good as can be expected, I suppose.

Apparently, he was trying to find his way to our place to see you when he got lost."

"Mason?" Lila prompted.

"Jake's got him," he told her. "He's fine."

A soft sob escaped her lips. "Can I talk to him?"

His brother must have heard her, because he said, "Finn's not ready to talk to his momma quite yet. I'll see what I can do during the ride back to the house."

"I'll let Momma and Violet know you're on your way. See you back at the house," he told his brother and then disconnected the call.

"Mason," she groaned, and he understood her need to talk to her son. To hear his voice and know that he was all right. He felt the same way. But he wasn't about to push his child into doing anything that would upset him more when they'd only just found him.

"Give him time, Lila," he told her. "He's on emotional overload tonight. Do you want to call Mrs. Tully and let her know we've found Finn?"

"She doesn't know he was missing," she told him. "She was already in bed when Finn and I went for a walk. I didn't want to wake her. Why cause her undue stress when I would find him soon enough? Only I didn't.

And ended up shocking and worrying your family instead."

"It wasn't the way I'd planned on telling them about Finn," he admitted, "but life doesn't always go as planned." He knew that better than most. "And getting back to you blaming yourself for what happened between us all those years ago, it takes two to make a baby." That said, he started back toward the house.

Lila followed, remaining a few steps behind. "But if it weren't for me, you wouldn't have been put in that position," she told him, her voice breaking. "You sinned that day because of me."

He stopped walking and turned to face her, the flashlight's beam casting enough light for him to see her face. "Lila, you'd just lost both your parents. Not weeks, months or even years apart. You lost them both the very same day."

She winced at the painful reminder.

Mason went on, "I sought to comfort you, because I loved you and it tore me up seeing the emotional pain you were in that day. We both got in over our heads. Instead of turning away from the Lord, you could have sought His forgiveness. Just as I did. Instead you ran and took my son away with you."

"I'm sorry," she said.

As if her regret would change anything, he thought, trying hard not to give in to the bitterness he felt over her betrayal of their love. "My son will know the Lord, Lila. In fact, I want him to join my family, *his* family, for church on Sundays while you're here in Sweet Springs."

"You don't even know if they're going to accept Finn as a part of their lives," she said worriedly.

"He's their flesh and blood," Mason reminded her. "Once they get over the initial shock of our having had a child out of wedlock when we were teens, I know they'll welcome him with open arms."

"I hope so," she said softly. "He deserves to be a part of a family who will love him. And he also deserves a chance to have the Lord in his life."

"So do you, Lila. With faith there can be forgiveness. That being said, if you'd like to accompany Finn when he joins us for church, I wouldn't object. No matter what's happened between us."

"I'm not sure I can," she answered. "But thank you for the invitation."

It saddened him that she had lost her faith. But accepting the Lord into one's life was a personal decision. Doing so would have to be up to Lila. "We'd best get back to the house." And to all the questions his family was bound to have.

"Thank you for helping us search for Finn," Lila told Jake when they arrived to find him waiting out on the porch for them.

"I did it for Mason," he muttered with a frown. "And for my nephew."

"Jake," Mason admonished.

"It's all right," Lila said. "I don't blame him for being upset with me."

"He's not helping the situation," Mason said, meeting his brother's angry gaze.

The front door opened, and Mrs. Landers poked her head out. "I thought I heard voices out here. Violet just took Finn to the kitchen to make him a peanut butter and marshmallow fluff sandwich." Her brows pinched together in worry as her gaze shifted to Lila. "Oh dear. He's not allergic to nuts, is he?"

"No," Lila said, shaking her head in response. "But you don't have to feed him. I can fix him something back at Mama Tully's."

"It's no bother," Mason's mother assured her. "Come on in. I'm sure you're anxious to see him." Obviously sensing the tension between her sons, she said, "Lila and I will be back out in a bit."

"He's my son, too," Lila heard Mason say as she started inside.

"Of course," his momma said. "That's going to take a bit of getting used to."

Anxious to see her son, Lila left them behind, hurrying to the kitchen. "Finn," she exclaimed in happy relief the moment she saw him seated at the table.

He looked her way, and she gasped, seeing a raised welt on one of his tear-streaked cheeks.

"The tip of a branch caught him," Violet told her as she grabbed a jar of marshmallow fluff from the pantry, carrying it over to the counter where she was preparing to make Finn's sandwich.

"Oh, honey," Lila groaned, reaching out to touch the raised line.

Finn pulled away from her touch, and it broke her heart.

"I put some ointment on it," Constance Landers said as she and Mason joined them in the kitchen. "Fortunately, the branch didn't break the skin."

"Thank you for tending to him," Lila replied, wanting so desperately to hug her son. To tell him that everything would be all right.

But would it? She had caused so many people she cared about emotional pain.

"You gave us a scare," Mason said as he approached his son.

Finn looked up at him in what looked like awe. "I was trying to find you."

"That's what I hear," he said with a nod. "Were you looking for me up a peach tree?" he asked, clearly trying to lighten the moment. Reaching out, he gently inspected his son's cheek.

Unlike he had with Lila, Finn didn't try to pull away. At seeing that, her aching heart squeezed even tighter.

"I wasn't in a tree. I tried to take a shortcut," Finn admitted with a frown. "I didn't see the branch hanging down in front of me."

"I know that," Mason replied with a calming smile. "But in the future, no more taking shortcuts through the orchard when it's dark. Stick to the path that runs between the rows of fruit trees. It'll make it easier to find your way back home."

Lila had to wonder if Mason realized he was giving his first piece of fatherly advice to their son. And then his gently spoken words settled in—*it'll make it easier to find your way back home*. How far into the future was Mason referring to? Did he mean during her and Finn's stay there? Did he mean whenever they would return for visits, because Finn deserved to spend time with his father and his father's family? Or did Mason intend to seek full custody of the son he'd been denied all these years? She couldn't blame him if he did, but she would fight with everything she had in her to keep her son in her life.

"Is this my home, too?" Finn asked, looking up at his father. "Since you're my dad."

"Finn—" Lila began, unsure what she'd even been about to say. Not that it mattered as Mason cut her off with his own reply.

"Absolutely."

"So I can stay here with you while we're here?" her son asked unsurely.

Mason looked to Lila as if unsure himself of what to say.

"Violet," Mrs. Landers said, "why don't we give Mason and Lila a little time alone to talk to Finn?"

"I don't want to talk to her," Finn muttered as he glanced Lila's way.

Lila's hurt at his response came out as a soft gasp.

"If you two don't mind," Mason said to his family.

"We don't," his momma said and started from the kitchen.

Setting the butter knife she'd just pulled from the kitchen drawer down next to the open jar of peanut butter, his sister gave a reluctant nod, cast a worried glance in Finn's direction and then followed their momma from the kitchen.

Lila moved to take a seat next to her son. "Honey, I'm so sorry that the choices I made when I found out I was having a baby have hurt you so deeply."

"You kept my daddy from me for my whole life!" her son blurted out, tears looming in his dark brown eyes.

"I know," she said shamefully as she took in her son's anguish through the sheen of her own tears.

Mason settled himself onto a chair across the table from them. "Son, I know you're still reeling from what your momma told you tonight, but the three of us need to talk this out. Need to find a way to get past all the hurt and move on."

There was no question as to why she had loved Mason, still harbored deep feelings for him, even after all these years. He was kind and compassionate, and where another man might have sought to exact revenge on her, Mason was doing his best to smooth things over between her and Finn.

"Will you be a part of my life from now on?" Finn asked anxiously, as if he truly feared Mason might change his mind about wanting to be his daddy. And why wouldn't he? He'd grown up believing his father hadn't wanted to be in their lives.

"Now and forever," Mason replied, his words choked with emotion. He flicked a glance in Lila's direction before focusing once more on his son. "I'm your daddy. There's nowhere else I'd rather be than in your life for the rest of mine."

Finn's worried expression relaxed, and a small smile crept across his face. "Can you teach me how to catch a baseball?"

Mason nodded, moisture filling his eyes. "It would be my pleasure. If you want, I can teach you how to do other things, too. Like how to fish, and how to plant and care for a vegetable garden. And, if you're interested, I'd be happy to teach you how to know when a peach is ripe for picking. That is, if you'd like to learn about harvesting."

"I would," Finn said with an enthusiastic bob of his head. "I like peaches."

Mason chuckled. "That's good, because growing peaches is a family tradition. Your great-grandpa planted the first of our family's orchard a long time ago. My daddy took it over from him. And now your uncle Jake, aunt Violet and I help with the running of this place, tending to the existing trees, creating new orchards, picking the fruit when harvest season arrives."

Finn sat listening intently, drawing on his daddy's every word.

"We can talk more about the orchard another time," Mason said, his tone growing more serious. "Right now, we need to address what happened tonight."

"I won't cut through the trees again when it's dark," Finn said apologetically.

"I know that," Mason assured him. "I'm referring to the talk your momma had with you. Like you, I'm not happy with how your momma chose to handle things when she found out we were going to have a baby. But we were young and hadn't gotten to the point where we made decisions, adult decisions, without some sort of guidance from either my momma and daddy or Mrs. Tully." Looking to Lila, he continued, "Life happened a bit out of order for us. We should have been married when we had you. Your momma and I had talked about getting married after we both had finished college. In fact, I intended to surprise her with an engagement ring that summer she disappeared. A token of my commitment to her. To us."

Lila's fingers flew to her lips.

Mason went on, his attention returning to their son, "After she left, I searched everywhere for her. Not just in Sweet Springs, but every town around ours, too. For months and months."

His words struck Lila hard, adding to the heavy burden of guilt she'd been carrying around for so many years. They also pierced her heart. Mason had loved her so deeply, as she had him, yet her actions had probably made him doubt she'd ever had feelings for him. Yet he'd searched for her so desperately.

"I still have your picture," she said.

Mason's gaze shifted in her direction. "What?"

"Your senior yearbook picture," she explained, lowering her gaze. "I still have it. I carry it with me everywhere I go." Frowning, she added, "Except for this evening. I hadn't expected to be away from Mama Tully's for any length of time."

"I'm hungry," Finn said, clearly done with the conversation. At least, any part of Lila's explanations and justifications.

Lila couldn't blame him for seeking an end to their discussion. He'd already been given more than most adults could process in one evening. "We can talk more later, or tomorrow."

"If you have any questions, don't hesitate to come to me," Mason told Finn. "But not without telling an adult where you're going first."

"Or me," Lila said anxiously.

Pushing away from the table, Mason rose to his feet. "I'll go get your aunt Violet. She can finish making you that sandwich while your momma and I talk to your gramma Landers and uncle Jake."

Lila glanced toward the counter where Violet had left the fixings for the sandwich she had been preparing to make for Finn. She wanted to protest, to stop Mason from leaving to get his sister. But she refrained from doing so. She needed to apologize to Mason's momma. To Jake and Violet as well, for that matter.

Moments later, Mason returned with his sister, who was clearly avoiding looking in Lila's direction.

Despite the unspoken anger simmering in Violet's eyes, Lila cast her a grateful smile. "Thank you, Violet. I won't be long." She looked to Finn. "We need to be getting back to Gramma Tully's. I'd hate for her to awaken and find us gone and cause her to worry."

Finn just nodded in response.

Mason inclined his head, and Lila followed him from the kitchen. "Momma is out on the porch."

"And Jake?" she asked as they made their way through the house.

"Taking a walk," he muttered.

"At this time of night?" she pressed, thinking about how dark it was out there, even for someone who knew their way around.

"He's taking some time to cool off," he told her as he reached for the front door. "Jake's not exactly in the most sympathetic mood right now, and I wasn't about to risk Finn overhearing any sort of confrontation between the two of you. My son's been through enough tonight."

Before she could respond, he swung the door open and stepped out onto the lit porch. Lila followed, easing the door shut behind her. Her stomach churned with growing anxiety, something she hadn't felt to this level since leaving Sweet Springs with her precious secret.

Mrs. Landers turned from where she stood at the edge of the porch, looking out into the night. Arms crossed tightly about herself, she looked past Mason to Lila. "I've been standing out here having a few words with the Lord tonight, praying for Him to help me understand how it is that I have a grandson I never knew about." Hurt and confusion wove their way through her words as she spoke. "But it appears He's busy taking care of matters elsewhere, because He's given me no answers."

"Mrs. Landers," Lila said, moving past Mason, "I know what a shock this must be for you. I'm so very sorry you had to find out about Finn the way you did this evening."

Her gaze locked with Lila's. "If you hadn't come home to be with Vera, would I have ever found out I had a grandson? Would my son have ever known he was a father?"

Lila bit at her bottom lip as she struggled for an answer. Finally, with a shake of her head, she said softly, "I don't know."

"Well, at least you have the ability to be honest when you choose to be."

"Momma…" Mason cut in.

"It's okay," Lila told him. "I deserve every bit of what your family's feeling right now. What you must be feeling, although you've been far more restrained with your emotions than…" She fell silent, trying to pull herself together.

"I loved her, Momma," Mason said, causing Lila's gaze to shift his way. "Neither of us meant for things to go the way they did that day. The day her momma and daddy were taken from this earth."

Lila bit back a sob, recalling that day with such clarity. Remembering the pain as that long-held dream of someday having her family together again was shattered with one single phone call. Closing her eyes, she fought to push the memories away.

Gentle arms folded around her, taking Lila by surprise. Her first thought was that it was Mason offering comfort to her, but as she came back to the moment, to the kind hug she was enfolded in, she realized it was Mrs. Landers who had stepped forward to soothe her pain.

"I'm sorry you ever had to go through that hurt," she said.

Lila shook her head. "No, I'm the one who's sorry. If I had stayed, I would have brought shame to him. To your family. To Mama Tully. Mason wouldn't have been able to follow in his daddy's shoes."

Mrs. Landers released her and took a step back. "Honey, Mason was never meant to follow his daddy into the service of the Lord. At least, not in the same way. I knew that from the time he was a young boy. His heart lay with this orchard. And with you. He just needed to discover that for himself."

"I won't ask for your forgiveness," Lila told them both. "I just ask that you don't hold my actions against my son."

"Our son," Mason corrected.

"*My* grandson," Mrs. Landers said. "And we would never blame Finn for something he had no part in. As for any of us moving past what you've done, whatever your reasons for doing so might have been, it's going to take time. Time to forgive. Time to rebuild the trust that's been broken. Time to come to terms with the fact that we missed out on over eight years of my grandson's life, a child my husband never had the chance to know. But with faith there is forgiveness. Trust in the Lord to help mend the emotional divide between you and those you've hurt."

The hurt and disappointment in her tone were every bit as effective. But they had also offered a glimmer of hope for a chance at forgiveness someday. The urge to reach out to the faith she'd walked away from so long ago was so strong, yet guilt and shame still had her doubting her ability to do so.

"Speaking of faith," Mason said determinedly, "Finn will be joining us for Sunday services while he's here."

His momma's serious expression softened as a smile drew the corners of her mouth upward. "That would be wonderful." She looked to Lila. "Will you be joining us?"

"I…uh…" she stammered uneasily.

"I've told her she's welcome to accompany *our* son when he joins us for church," Mason answered for her.

Lila nodded. "Thank you for offering to include me."

"After what she's done, you're including her in our lives?"

Heads turned toward the shadowy figure striding toward the porch. Jake.

"I think it would be best if Finn joined you for church without me," Lila said. Her attending Sunday services with them would clearly cause discomfort for Jake and possibly Violet. She wouldn't add to the upset by being where she wasn't wanted. Where she wasn't even sure she would be comfortable.

"Jake," Mrs. Landers said as her youngest son stepped up onto the porch, "we need to focus on what's best for Finn. And if having Lila with him at church makes him more comfortable, then you will need to find a way to set your anger aside. At least for those few hours."

Jake bristled, jaw clenching. Then gave a curt nod of acquiescence. "For my nephew's sake, I'll leave the past out of God's house."

"Finn and I should get going," Lila said. "Mama Tully might wake up and need something."

"I'll go get him," Mrs. Landers offered.

"I'll come with you," Jake said.

"Jake," Lila called out as he started after his momma.

Pausing, he turned to look at her.

"I'm so sorry for all the hurt I've caused you and your family. I hope that someday you might find it in your heart to forgive me."

"Save your requests for forgiveness for church," he stated and then walked away.

She would do that as well, even though she wasn't sure if the Lord would welcome her back any more than Jake had.

"I'll talk to him," Mason said behind her.

"No," she said, shaking her head. "I will. After the shock of this evening's events eases, I'll try again. The same with Violet. They may never accept my apology, but I need to extend it to them all the same." And to her son, as well. She'd hurt him so deeply. Broken his trust. The look on his face after he'd learned the truth had really brought things home for her. In making the decisions she had, she'd taken so very much away from herself and Finn.

The screen door opened, and Finn stepped

outside with the grandmother he'd never known.

"He just finished eating his peanut butter and marshmallow sandwich."

"What do you tell…" Lila began, and then realized she had no idea how Mrs. Landers would want Finn to refer to her.

"Gramma Landers works just fine," the older woman supplied. "And he's already thanked Violet and me."

Lila looked to her son. "Well, then we'd best get going while there's a speck of moonlight out to guide us."

"You're not walking," Mason cut in. "Those clouds could shift again at any moment and leave you both wandering about the orchard in the dark. I'll take you home."

Home. Oh, how she wished it still were. But she had given that right up the day she'd run off.

Chapter Five

The ringing of her cell phone drew Lila's focus from her work emails. Closing the lid of her laptop, she picked up her phone.

"Addy," she said, wishing her friend and foster sister was there in person to talk to. But she would be soon.

"Good morning," Addy said on the other end of the line. "I thought I would wait until Finn left for church before calling, but I can't remember what time exactly Sunday service starts."

"It doesn't start until 10:30 a.m. Mama Tully is still getting ready, and Finn is letting the dogs out before we go," Lila said, her gaze drifting to the nearby window where she had a view of her son. It had been five days since Finn had learned the truth about Mason being his daddy. Today would be Finn's first

Sunday service ever and her first time back in church since leaving Sweet Springs all those years ago.

"We?" Addy repeated.

"I'm going with them," Lila said, trying to ignore the growing whirl of nerves in the pit of her stomach. No matter how anxious she was about stepping through those double doors of the church she'd once found comfort in, she would do so for her son, and to start righting the wrongs she'd done in her past.

"You are?" Addy said in surprise. "I'm so glad. When we spoke on the phone the other day, you weren't certain you would be able to do this."

"I'm still not," Lila admitted, "but I'm going anyway."

"We used to love going there with Mama Tully."

"That was so long ago," Lila said with a troubled frown. "To be honest—" because she had always been that with Addy "—I'm scared."

"It's not as if lightning is going to strike you down for stepping into the Lord's house," Addy teased. Cultivating a sense of humor was how Addy had learned to cope with her childhood, when she'd been living out of her mother's car. It was either laugh or cry, and

Addy had felt the need to be strong for her momma, so she'd held back the tears. Lila hadn't been able to keep her own tears at bay completely, letting them fall when she was alone in her room at night. But in the light of day she reined in her emotions for her son's sake.

"Maybe not physical lightning," Lila agreed. "But there will definitely be some emotional lightning going on inside that church this morning. Not only between Mason's family and myself, but with all those attending who will no doubt be shocked to learn Mason Landers has a son."

"There's bound to be lot of questions," Addy agreed. "But I doubt many of them will be asked while Finn is there. You just have to take this one day at a time and never forget that you didn't keep your son from him all these years to hurt Mason. You did it because you loved him."

"If only I could make Mason understand the why of it."

Her friend groaned in frustration. "I wish I could be there with you."

"Me, too," Lila replied, the words choked with emotion. "But you will be. Just a few more days."

"About that…"

"Addy, no," she gasped. "Please tell me you're still coming."

"I am, but not as soon as I'd hoped to," her friend replied. "Karen called me last night to give a verbal notice. Not a two-week notice, but an 'I'm quitting today' kind of notice that puts me back to square one."

"Why did she quit? I thought she liked it there." Karen was Addy's assistant pastry chef. Addy had been training her to step in and run things.

"She did, but she received a head pastry chef offer out of the blue at one of Atlanta's upscale country clubs. They needed someone who could start right away, leaving her no time to give notice," Addy explained. "So now I'll be training a new hire to take over for Karen and, hopefully, he'll be able to cover for me when I come to Sweet Springs. But it could be a month or more before that happens now. I'm just sorry that all of Mama Tully's care is falling to you."

"I don't mind," Lila told her. "I've already told you that Finn and I had no other plans this summer. Besides, Mama Tully is getting stronger every day. And you know her—she insists on doing everything herself. Not that I always sit back and allow her to. Even Mason refuses to let her tend to her garden yet."

"At least the two of you are on the same page when it comes to Mama Tully," her friend replied.

"I hadn't considered that," Lila agreed. "If only I knew where his thoughts stood where Finn is concerned." One thing that wasn't up in the air was Finn's thoughts toward her. Her son was nowhere ready to forgive her, but she held out hope that he would come around.

Her gaze shifted, taking in the smile on her son's face as he followed the pups back to the house. A smile he was far less free with when she was around. Her son's forgiveness might be the hardest of all to attain.

"You might start by asking him."

The knot in her stomach tightened. "I'm not sure I want to know."

"This isn't going to go away," her friend stated, as if Lila needed to be reminded of it. "Especially with Mason living right next door to you all summer."

Lila sighed. "I don't want to lose my son."

"Then don't. Talk to Mason. Work things out with him."

Addy was right. She was no longer the young, frightened girl who solved problems by running away from them. She was an adult. A mother whose son would learn from her actions. All the more reason to face the emotional turmoil she'd caused and do whatever she could to set things right. And to do that, she and Mason would need to interact more, set aside their past to focus on their son. While she and Mason had crossed paths on occasion, they hadn't spent any real time talking things over and she understood why. Like her son, Mason was hurting.

"Honey, it's almost time to go."

Lila glanced toward the living room entryway, where Mama Tully stood in her Sunday best. "I'm ready," she assured her. At least, as ready as she'd ever be. "I was just talking to Addy."

"Hi, sweetie," their foster mother called out.

"Give her my love," Addy said on the other end of the line.

"She sends her love," Lila repeated.

"I'll let you go," Addy said. "Call me later."

"I will." Disconnecting the call, Lila looked up at her foster mother. "Are you sure you're up for this? You've only just gotten home from the hospital."

"It's been days," Mama Tully said with a swipe of her hand, waving away Lila's worry.

"Not long enough for you to be overdoing things."

"I'm not going to be tending my garden or

chasing Honey and Grits around the yard. I'll be sitting in a pew at church."

Lila supposed she was worrying needlessly. Mama Tully wouldn't be overexerting herself just sitting there in church, listening to that morning's sermon. Even so, she'd make certain to find them seats in one of the rear pews. That way, if Mama Tully started feeling poorly during the service, they could slip out without causing any noticeable disruption. Her real hesitation in going had more to do with what she'd admitted to Addy. She was afraid. Church or not, so many would judge her once the truth was out. Judge her actions. Judge her morals. Maybe even judge her as a parent, as so many had done her mother. And though her and her momma's situations had been completely different, both she and her parents had caused their children emotional pain.

Mama Tully settled herself onto the floral sofa cushion beside her, placing a comforting hand over Lila's. "Don't let your thoughts carry you away to places you're better off not visiting."

"How did you know?" Lila asked with a sad smile.

"I mothered you for several years," the older woman replied. "Back when you were sad and scared and always expecting the worse. Not that anyone could blame you after the life you'd had up until that point." She gave Lila's hand a gentle squeeze. "What I'm trying to say is don't let the past come back to undo all the good you've done with your life. You are not your mother."

Tears pricked at the backs of Lila's eyes. "Thank you for saying that."

"Why wouldn't I?" Mama Tully said with a loving smile. "It's the truth. Sure, there are a few wrongs that need to be righted, but I have faith you will see it done. And if it takes another week, even two, for you to be ready to step inside that church again, then so be it. I'm sure Finn and I can ride into town with Mason."

A week or two wasn't going to change anything. Lila knew that. Forgiveness might never come from Mason and his family, and she would have to accept that. Although she prayed it would someday. She also needed the Lord's forgiveness for having forsaken Him for so long. Needed to be there that morning for her son's introduction to the Lord…and her own reintroduction.

Lila shook her head. "This is something I need to do. But thank you for understanding."

Warmth filled the older woman's smile. "I

know you're a grown woman, so you're past needing my guidance. But I can offer you my support along with a willing ear whenever you have the need to talk."

"I will never be too old to appreciate your words of guidance," Lila told her, meaning it with all her heart. Mama Tully was the only mother her heart had ever known.

"I'll keep that in mind." With another gentle squeeze of Lila's hand, Mama Tully eased to her feet. "I'll be sure to offer up a prayer for you during this morning's services, asking the Lord to see you through the emotionally difficult days you have ahead of you with Mason."

"I'm pretty sure the Lord is going to be taking Mason's side in this," Lila stated as she pushed to her feet.

"Now, Lila," Mama Tully said in a gently scolding voice, "the Lord doesn't take sides. He loves us all equally. Now, go get your purse. I'll be out on the porch with Finn."

She looked to the older woman, a sense of panic filling her. "But I shut God out of my life for more than nine years."

"All you have to do is open up the door to your heart, to your faith, and let Him in." Turning, she walked from the room, leaving Lila to reflect on her words of guidance.

* * *

They were the last to arrive at church, having had to run back to the house to grab Mama Tully's Bible. She'd accidentally left it lying atop the kitchen table when she'd gone in there to get a handful of treats for Honey and Grits before leaving. Thankfully, the rain the weather station had called for that morning had held off. Mama Tully didn't need to be traipsing about in foul weather in her somewhat weakened condition.

Mason stood just outside the church doors, dressed in a button-down shirt and navy dress pants. The expression he wore was nearly as dark as the clouds looming overhead. No doubt he believed it was her fault they had barely made it there only moments before that morning's service was set to begin. Not that she could blame him.

Lila's gaze moved past Mason to the open pair of wooden doors, and panic flickered to life in her stomach. She had bigger worries to focus on at that moment than Mason's accusatory stare. She was about to face God.

Finn broke into a run toward the church and his awaiting daddy.

Relief replaced the angry expression on Mason's face as his attention shifted to the boy racing toward him. His son. Had he thought Lila would go against her word and keep their son from attending that morning?

Mama Tully stepped in close to her. "You can do this," she whispered supportively.

With a nod, Lila raised her chin and then, slipping her arm through her foster mother's, started in the direction of the church.

Mason had just reached out to affectionately tousle Finn's hair when she reached them. Letting his hand fall away, he looked to Lila. "Jake and Violet are saving seats for us. Momma just went in to take hers."

"I'll go on in," Mama Tully said, slipping her arm free of Lila's. "See you all inside," she said as she left Lila standing there with the two men she loved most in the world. The same two who would probably prefer her to be anywhere else but standing there with them.

"Addy called as we were getting ready to leave," Lila said, feeling the need to break the uncomfortable silence.

"You're here," he said flatly, looking once more to his son. "That's all that matters." Then, inclining his head, Mason said, "We'd best get in there. Reverend Hutchins will be starting his sermon soon."

"You go first," Lila said. "We'll follow."

But Finn didn't follow. Instead, he started

up the center aisle, practically pinned to his daddy's side. Every single pew was filled and rippling with that Sunday-morning exuberance Lila remembered from so long ago. She slowed her step, searching the back pews for Mama Tully. Mason, however, continued moving forward, as did Finn. Before Lila could call her son back, to inform him they would be taking their seats at the back of the church, she caught sight of Mama Tully waving to her from the very front pew.

In addition to things already not going as planned, her foster mother was seated next to Mason's family, talking with Mrs. Landers. Violet briefly met her gaze and then turned away. Jake, as she'd expected, chose not to even acknowledge her presence. More and more curious gazes turned her way with each advancing step she took. Open chatter quickly dropped to muffled whispers, causing Lila's heart to pound all the more fiercely in her chest. Nothing less than she deserved, but she continued onward. Forgiveness from the Lord lay in this moment, in her willingness to face up to what she had done. For herself. For her son. For all those she loved.

Mason nodded in every direction, offering morning greetings and hellos as he went, just as he had done every Sunday service when they were teens, as if he hadn't a care in the world. Didn't he realize the ramifications of what they were about to do? And why did they have to choose that day of all days to sit in the front row, where every single pair of eyes would be upon them? They never sat that far forward. Or, at least, they hadn't when she'd lived in Sweet Springs. She'd changed. She supposed others could have as well, since she'd been gone, in both mind-sets and everyday routines. She prayed that were the case, because she couldn't bear the thought of them judging her son because of the choices she'd made.

Mason stopped next to his family's chosen pew, bent to say something in Finn's ear and then turned, waiting for her to catch up. When she did, he casually extended a hand, motioning her to take her place in the pew. "After you," he offered up with a surprisingly warm smile.

Pinning her gaze to the wine-colored carpet beneath her feet, she stepped past him and eased down onto the pew next to Mama Tully. Mason sent Finn into the row after her and then promptly settled his six-foot frame onto the end of the pew, nearest the center aisle.

The only good thing about almost being late for Sunday service was that there had been no time to mingle with the rest of the congregation beforehand. No time to be asked or to have to answer questions.

The organ music ceased playing as a man Lila could only assume was Reverend Hutchins stepped up to the pulpit, a welcoming smile on his time-worn face. "Good morning," he called out into the microphone in front of him.

His greeting was promptly returned in unison by those attending that morning's service.

"It's so good to see so many of you here today. Especially Vera Tully," he added, looking Mama Tully's way.

She nodded in response, her fingers curled lovingly around the edges of the worn Bible she'd carried with her to church ever since Lila had first met her foster mother.

"God does listen to our prayers," the reverend said to all those seated before him.

"Amen" was muttered throughout the pews.

"Today's sermon," he began, "is about not casting judgment. I decided on this topic after a lengthy discussion last evening with Mason Landers." He directed his kind gaze to Mason. "Mason has asked if he might say a few words before I begin this morning's service. Son," he prompted, stepping aside.

"Mason?" Lila gasped softly as he stood

and moved toward the podium. She sat forward, as if to run after him. To stop him from whatever he was about to say.

"Let him go, dear," Mama Tully said in a whisper.

"What is he doing?" she said, panic rising inside her. Was he going to condemn her in front of more than half the town? While her son—no, their son—sat looking on? Finn hadn't asked for any of this. She prayed Mason's resentment wouldn't blind him to the hurt his actions could cause their son.

"He's doing what needs doing," Mrs. Landers said softly, her focus resting on her son. "That's why we're all seated here together. To show our support."

Mason cleared his throat, drawing Lila's panicked gaze back to the pulpit, behind which he now stood looking out over the hushed crowd. "Nine years ago," he began, and Lila felt the palms of her clenched hands moisten, "I sought forgiveness for a moment of weakness. One that came about because I sought to give comfort to the girl I loved."

The girl who had loved him. Still loved him, she thought sadly.

"The girl I had intended to marry," he went on, his deep voice filling the room.

"I think he's talking about you, Momma," Finn said, his gaze pinned on his daddy.

"And though it's true that I veered off the spiritual path that I had walked upon my entire life, the Lord did not set me aside," he said, looking to Lila. "Because God is forgiving. So much so, despite my sin, He saw fit to bless me with a son."

Shocked gasps and muted whispers moved like a wildfire on a windy day throughout the congregation.

Mason looked to Finn, a tender expression moving across his tanned face. "I'd like to thank Reverend Hutchins for allowing me this opportunity to introduce my son to all of you. I pray you will make Finn feel every bit a part of this town as you have me."

The reverend stepped up beside Mason, placing a supportive hand on his broad shoulder. "I have no doubt they will. Thank you for trusting us with your truth."

Guilt sliced through Lila.

As Mason returned to his seat, Reverend Hutchins returned to his place behind the podium. His focus was on Finn. "I'd like to be the first to welcome you to our church, Finn, and to Sweet Springs, as well." Then he looked to Lila. "Welcome back to the Lord's house. We're glad to have you here."

"Thank you," she replied.

Words of welcome rose up from the surrounding pews, filling the sanctuary.

At their kind words Lila turned her head to glance down at her son. Joy was written all over Finn's face. He'd wanted a father of his own and all that came with it for as long as Lila could remember. And now Finn had that and so much more.

Somewhat sheepishly, her son returned the reverend's smile. "Thank you for having me," Finn replied, in not quite the booming voice of his father, but loud enough to be heard throughout the room. "Is this when I get to send a prayer up to God to thank Him for giving me a daddy *and* a new family?"

Lila's heart tugged at her son's request. God had given her son the family she hadn't been able to. Because the only way to have given him more, other than returning to Sweet Springs and confessing her long-held secret, was to marry and have more children. But marriage had never been a viable option for her. Not when her heart had long ago been given to Mason.

Her gaze lifted from Finn's beaming face to find Mason, a man of fairly controlled emotion, holding back tears, a knot of emotion bobbing up and down in his throat. On the other side of Mama Tully, Mrs. Landers was sniffling softly and dabbing a tissue to her eyes. Jake and Violet held hands in silent support as they looked on.

Reverend Hutchins smiled down from his pulpit. "The Lord welcomes any words you feel the need to share with him, now or anytime you feel the need to speak to Him. Be it here, or at home, or wherever you may be."

Finn nodded and then looked up at his daddy. "I'd like to tell him now, if that's okay. While we're in God's house. Because He gave me the best present I could ever ask for."

Lila felt a huge piece of her son's love slipping away from her in that moment. A piece that hadn't rightfully been hers to begin with, but it hurt all the same. *Lord*, she found herself praying silently, *please help me to be strong*.

"Mason."

He turned as his momma stepped out onto the back porch, where he'd stood for a long while looking out over the nearby orchard following Sunday service that morning.

"Your lunch is getting cold," she said, concern written all over her face.

"I'm not hungry."

She nodded in understanding. "I'll cover

your plate and put it in the refrigerator. You can eat it whenever you feel up to it."

After that morning's service, Mason had stayed behind to field several expected questions from their closest friends, while everyone else had returned home, Lila and Finn included. His son had wanted to remain behind with him, but his tender ears needed no more detail than what he already knew about the situation. At Finn's age, vague was enough. Someday, however, it might be a different story. Some Mason's to tell. Some Lila's.

His heart felt relief at having the truth out, yet rehashing the past that morning had played havoc on both his mind and his heart. There had been a time that he'd imagined what it would be like to attend Sunday services with his very own family, Lila and any children they might have had. That time had finally come, although not at all as he had pictured it. Even so, his son was there to share in his faith, just as Mason had his own daddy's. And he was grateful Lila had chosen to accompany their son that morning. It couldn't have been easy for her, but it was a start toward the healing that needed to take place between all of them.

"I'd appreciate it," he replied, hating that he

was causing her to worry needlessly. He was a grown man. He would be fine. "I just need to spend a little time out here, taking in the fresh air and sorting through my thoughts."

"No doubt you have a great deal weighing on you right now," she acknowledged. "Finding out that I have a grandson hasn't quite settled fully into my mind yet, either."

"Thank you for offering your support at church this morning. You, Jake and Violet."

"Honey, we're family. Finn, too," she added with a smile. "We stick together. I'm just glad Lila decided to attend this morning's service."

Mason looked to her in surprise. "You wanted her there?"

His momma nodded and then crossed the porch to a planter. "I wanted my grandson to join us, something that might not have happened if Lila chose not to attend," she said as she reached up to pluck a handful of wilted flowers off the potted petunia.

He shook his head. "That wasn't going to happen. Lila knows where I stand on the matter. Our son was going to attend church this morning, with or without her."

Stepping away from the porch railing, his momma turned to face him. "Even though Finn is hurt, she's still that boy's momma. The only person he truly knows here in Sweet

Springs. It stands to reason he'd feel more at ease with her by his side, so, yes, I was glad to see her there."

"I suppose you're right," he said grudgingly. Finn was dealing with so much as it was. He didn't want him to feel uncomfortable or pressured in any way.

"She's trying, Mason," Constance said, her tone gentle. "I can only imagine the amount of courage it took for Lila to step through those doors today, knowing she'd wronged so many who cared for her. As much courage, I would say, as it took for you to stand in front of the congregation this morning and tell your story."

He nodded. It had been hard, but it had been done in his son's best interest. He'd done it for the girl he'd once known and loved. The woman he still harbored feelings for, no matter how deeply she had hurt him.

"I've never been so proud of you," his momma went on. "I know your daddy would have been, too."

Mason wasn't so sure about that, but he'd take his momma's word for it. She'd known his father far longer than he had. His parents had been married for going on twenty-five years when his daddy passed.

"I thought about him last night," Mason

said, the emotional admission adding rasp to his voice.

"You did?" his momma replied with a heartfelt smile.

"I thought about all the talks we had when I was growing up," he told her. "About all the sermons I'd heard Daddy give. About how much I wish he was still here to talk to, because I know he'd offer me guidance when it comes to finding it in myself to forgive Lila for what she did. Then I lay awake, praying for God to help me find the right words to speak in front of this morning's congregation. Praying even harder that my son would be accepted by those I've known all my life."

Looking up at him, her expression tender. "As Reverend Hutchins said this morning, God does listen to our prayers."

Not always, he wanted to say, but he left the words where they lay, just beyond his tongue. God had given him the greatest gift of all.

"Your words were spoken from the heart, they were repentant and honest, and while you had the opportunity to cast Lila in a very poor light, you didn't." His momma went back to sprucing up her petunias. "That, to me, is the beginning of forgiveness."

"I was protecting my son by protecting her." But the truth was he couldn't bring himself to intentionally cause her pain,. Not when his feelings for her, much to his chagrin, still occupied such a large part of his heart. These emotions had only reawakened with her return.

His momma looked up at him with that knowing look only a mother could give. "And not because a part of you still cares for Lila?"

"We were over a long time ago," he countered with a frown.

"The two of you have a son together," she said. "It'll never be over completely. Finn will always be that shared connection between the two of you. But since you're over the feelings you once had for Lila, something only you could know because it's your heart that had once been so deeply invested in her, it'll make things a bit easier for you two to talk with calm, clear heads."

"I'm over *her*, not over what she did to me. It's not something I'm sure I will ever be able to get past."

"Mason," she said empathetically.

"I loved her, Momma. Intended to marry her, and it had nothing to do with taking responsibility for my actions. Our actions. But instead of the happily-ever-after life together I'd conjured up in my mind for us, she ran off without ever looking back."

"She loved you, Mason," his momma said tenderly. "I saw it in her eyes whenever the two of you were together. I can't begin to tell you why she did what she did. Only she can do that. That said, I'll leave you to your fresh air. Holler if you need anything." She moved to place a kiss on his cheek. "I'm not your daddy, but I am here for you anytime you need to talk."

A warm smile tugged at his mouth. "I love you, Momma."

"Love you, too."

After she'd gone, Mason's thoughts went back to Lila.

I still have your picture. That unexpected admission, he thought with a heavy sigh, had reached right into his closed-off heart. *I carry it with me everywhere I go.*

He didn't want to think about what that meant. It was easier to feel the anger than the hurt. Easier to believe she'd never loved him than to consider the possibility that she had done what she'd done for his sake. Because to do so filled him with all the what-ifs he'd rather not contemplate. Like, what if she had come to him when she'd found out they were going to have a baby? Trusted him to stand by her side, working through whatever hardships they might have faced together? What if he'd proposed to her sooner and had been able to reassure her that he loved her and wanted to spend the rest of his life with her? What if he'd made more effort to convince her that he wasn't like her daddy, who had walked away when Lila's momma told him she was pregnant with his child?

Lila's parents had eventually gotten back together, but not for Lila's sake. It had been over their mutual love of illegal substances. But Finn would never have to deal with anything like that, Mason vowed. Never.

"Grits!" Lila shrieked as she reached for the shoe the naughty pup had taken from the porch, only to lose her footing on the wet earth of Mama Tully's garden. Down she went into a face-first slide between the collard greens and the potatoes, taking a few unfortunate pieces of vegetation with her as she went.

"Lila?" a voice boomed. The slapping sound of booted footsteps crossing the rain-soaked garden followed. A second later, Mason's large form was kneeling next to her. "Are you okay?"

Anybody but him, she thought to herself as she lay trying to catch her breath. Grits, apparently realizing the chase was over, scampered over to stand in front of Lila. She could see his muddied paws through the strands of hair hanging limply over her face.

"Lila?" Mason repeated with more urgency.

A shoe dropped onto the rain-soaked ground in front of her. *Her* shoe. The whole reason she was lying there in utter embarrassment. As much as she'd like to continue to lie there in silence, wishing Mason away, Lila knew there was no possibility of that happening. Pushing up onto her elbows, feeling the ooze of damp earth and rainwater soak even deeper into her clothes, Lila replied, "I think so." Then, glancing back over her shoulder with a frown, added, "I'm not so sure Mama Tully's potato plants are, though."

He responded with a soft chuckle as he followed the line of her gaze. "That was definitely a major league–level home plate slide, if ever. Thankfully, the collard greens were spared. The potatoes are ready to be picked anyway, and you only mangled a few plants, so no real harm was done." His attention swung back around to her. "Speaking of harm, are you sure you're all right?"

"Other than being beyond embarrassed and having a dress that will probably never make its way into a church again—" she paused to look at the muddy shoe in front of her "—

make that dress *and* shoes, I'm just peachy."
At least, she hoped she was. There was far
too much distraction, Mason's being there in
particular, to really be able to do a full assess-
ment for any injuries. It had been two weeks
since she'd returned to church, and, in that
time, Mason had been coming around more
often to spend time with Finn, including her
in some of their outings, as well. That was
something he hadn't been obligated to do, but
the kindness touched her deeply. Made her
wish for what she could never have again—
Mason's love.

"I think you're right about this shoe's fate,"
Mason said with a grin. Reaching out, Mason
plucked it from the mud and then stood. Then
he extended his other hand to her.

Lila felt as if she was going back in time
as she reached for his offered hand and felt
his fingers close around hers. It was something Mason had done countless times when
she'd lived there. Following long talks under
their peach tree, he would always help her to
her feet. Only she'd usually been in a sitting
position, not sprawled across the dirt. And
Mason had done so not only because he'd
been raised to be a gentleman, as he was no
doubt doing right now, but because he'd loved
her back then.

Grits barked and danced around them as Mason helped Lila to her feet. She rocked unsteadily as her bare feet sank into the mud.

"I've got you," Mason said, sliding a supportive arm around her waist. Rain came down harder, streaming down his face as he looked at her. "We'd best get back to the house. I think we're in for a lengthy downpour."

She nodded, trying not to think about how it felt to have his strong arm wrapped around her. "I think you're right."

Together, they hurried back to the house, making it onto the porch only moments before the clouds opened up fully. The deluge of rain cast a thick curtain between them and Mama Tully's front yard.

"Made it just in time," Mason remarked.

Lila glanced down at her muddied self. "Maybe I should have stayed out in the yard. The rain could only have helped me."

"I would ask what you were doing outside in the garden in this weather," he said as they shook the excess rainwater from their hair and limbs, "but I think the shoe Grits attempted to gift you with answers that question." He held the wet, mud-covered wedge sandal up between them.

"That used to be one of my favorites."

"I feel like I can safely say it's not going to be any longer," he teased, just as naturally as he once had.

She shook her head. "If I had known he had a thing for shoes…"

"Ahh," he said with a nod of understanding. "Grits here decided to play a game of catch me if you can, using your shoe as a lure."

"That pretty much covers it," she agreed. "Mama Tully went inside to start fixing lunch and Finn took Honey to find her ball. I stayed out on the porch to take in some fresh air and mull over this morning's sermon while I sat watching the storm roll in. My mistake was in taking off my dress sandals. The rest, as they say, is history."

Grits chose that moment to shake the water and mud from himself.

With a startled squeal, Lila took cover behind Mason.

Sputtering as the water sprayed across the front of him from his head down to his toes, Mason groaned, "Grits!"

When Lila decided it was safe to come out of hiding, she burst into laughter. "Maybe you and I should both step out into the rain to rinse all of this mud off us."

"Momma…"

They both turned toward the sound of their son's voice.

Pushing the screen door open, Finn stepped outside with Honey at his heels. The pup adored him, choosing to stay at Finn's side while Grits was off doing his own thing more often than not. That day's thing just happened to be swiping her shoe.

Finn smiled wide the second he caught sight of Mason standing there on the porch. "Daddy!" That happy expression faltered slightly. "Is it okay if I call you that?"

The corners of Mason's mouth tilted upward. "It's more than okay, son. I'd like nothing more."

Lila's heart melted at both Mason's response and the joy that moved across their son's face with his reply.

It was then Finn took notice of his father's rain-soaked state. "Why are you all wet and muddy?"

"I got caught out in the rain." He looked to the dog. "And then Grits here decided to give me a mud bath."

Finn's brows drew together in confusion.

"It's a saying," Lila explained. "Grits was muddy and shook, spraying it all over your daddy."

Her son looked her over. "Is that why you're so muddy?"

"No, I was already muddy. I fell in the garden while I was chasing Grits," she explained as she pushed the damp curls from her face.

"This ornery mutt stole your momma's shoe," Mason said as he reached down to scratch the panting pup behind his ear.

"Then how come you're the one holding it?" their son asked. Of course, Grits, the rascal, sat there, looking completely innocent of any wrongdoing.

Mason chuckled. "You don't miss a thing, do you?"

Lila couldn't help but smile. "I slipped in the vegetable garden when I was chasing Grits, and your daddy came to my rescue."

"Not soon enough," Mason acknowledged as he took in the sight of her.

"I should go get cleaned up," Lila said, growing slightly chilled in her damp clothes.

"Would you mind if I stuck around a bit to visit with Finn?" Mason asked.

Finn jumped right in. "Can he, Momma? Please?"

She looked to Mason. "Don't you want to get home and get into something dry?"

"It can wait," he replied. "I know I should

have called first to make sure you didn't mind my coming over."

"There's no need," she told him. They had never called first when she used to live there. It wasn't that far of a walk between houses if their visit ended up being poorly timed. She saw no reason to require a call from him first now. He had every right to see his son when he wanted to. "You're welcome to stop by and see Finn anytime."

He nodded. "I appreciate that. Especially since I'd have to walk home in that," he said, glancing beyond the shelter of the porch's roof to where the storm continued.

"You're welcome to come inside," she offered.

"And drip all over Mrs. Tully's floors?" he said, looking down at his wet clothes. "Better not. But thank you for the invite. Finn and I will make use of these porch chairs."

"If you're sure," she said and started for the door. Pausing just inside, she glanced back. "And Mason…"

He looked her way. "Yes?"

"Thank you for coming to my rescue." She smiled at the memory of it.

"You're welcome."

Lila left them to their visit, something she wished she could be a part of. She'd missed the talks she and Mason used to have on this same porch. The playful conversations that had verged on beyond silly at times. Conversations her son would now be able to share with his daddy. And for that she was beyond grateful, because Finn's happiness meant the world to her. As did Mason's.

Mason and Finn settled themselves into the matching rockers, watching the rain fall. "I'm sorry I didn't have a chance to really talk to you after church this morning."

"It's okay," his son said. "Momma said you wanted to but couldn't get away from all the people asking you questions about me."

He appreciated Lila assuring Finn that he'd had other intentions where his son was concerned. "My having a son came as quite a shock to everyone."

"Are they mad at my momma, too?"

"I'm not mad at her," Mason said. "Well, maybe a little," he said, preferring to be honest with his son. But at the same time, he didn't want to draw Finn into his and Lila's issues. He was a young boy, deserving of a carefree life. He and Lila were adults, ones who had a lot of complicated issues to work through, despite their brief moment of shared laughter. "But I'm working on it." It was hard to hold on to the anger when his heart had finally come back to life after so many years.

"I'm mad at her," Finn declared with a pinched frown.

"Finn, I understand why you might be upset with your momma," Mason began, "but we all have to figure out a way to let go of our anger. Otherwise, it'll fester inside us and keep us from appreciating all the good things we have in our lives. And as far as other people being upset with your momma, I don't think they are. They're mostly just trying to take all of this in."

"Uncle Jake is mad at her," Finn stated matter-of-factly. "Aunt Violet, too, but she still says hello."

Mason nodded, hating that Finn was picking up on his siblings' conflicted emotions. He was still harboring some resentment toward Lila himself, but he did his best to keep those emotions firmly tucked away whenever Finn was around. His family needed to put Finn's happiness first, and slighting Lila was not at all conducive to that. Nor was it the Christian thing to do. In his heart, he knew that he would forgive Lila. It was the right thing to do. Because of Finn, but also because he still loved her. He'd tried not to, but his heart refused to cooperate.

Mason shifted in the porch chair to face his son. "Your aunt Violet and your uncle Jake are hurt that they missed so many years of your growing up. It's something they're going to have to work through. Something all of us are working through," he said honestly. "But it will get better." He'd see that it did.

"I like it here."

One corner of Mason's mouth pulled upward. "I'm glad. I know you live in Alabama, but I want you to know that Sweet Springs will always be your home, too."

"Can I come live here with you?"

This wasn't a subject he'd been prepared to delve into. Not until he'd spoken to Lila about how they would work out custody arrangements. "I think your momma would be really sad if you were to live so far away from her."

Finn's smile drooped.

"We'll figure something out," Mason assured him. "Maybe you can spend your summers here. And some of your holiday breaks."

Fortunately, his response managed to spark some life back into his son, as dark brown eyes that mirrored Mason's own lifted to him full of hope. "Or maybe Momma and me can move here to live. And then I would have all my family with me all the time."

If only life were that simple, Mason thought

to himself. And his was anything but. "I can't make you any promises," he said honestly. "But your momma and I will work together to come up with a plan that has your best interest in mind." He prayed he could figure out a way to keep both Lila and Finn a part of his future, because his life felt blessedly complete with them in it.

Chapter Six

My time here is coming to an end far too *quickly,* Lila thought with a sad sigh as she reached into the back seat of her car to grab the two bags of groceries she and Mama Tully had picked up after church. Mama Tully was nearly back to full strength and summer was more than half over. Addy would be coming soon, while she and Finn would be heading home to Alabama. She would miss the days spent sitting with Mama Tully on the porch, reminiscing about the past. Miss the moments she'd shared with Mason and Finn, laughing and playing. Miss church and picking peaches and the life she'd almost had. Nudging the car door closed with her hip, she followed Mama Tully into the house.

"Well," Mama Tully said as she set her purse along with the half gallon of milk she'd carried in down atop the hall table, "that was truly an inspiring sermon."

While Lila had attended church services for the past three Sundays, she had still been struggling to get past the guilt and find her way back to the Lord. That morning's service had moved something inside her, though. She realized she needed the Lord in her life, needed to know she could turn to Him in prayer in times of strife. Needed to know that He was watching over her son, which she now realized He was.

"So heartwarming," Lila agreed as she walked over to let Grits and Honey out of their room. A family of five from the next town over who had lost their home in a recent fire had attended that morning's service. Though they were not members of this church, they had expressed their gratitude for the monetary contributions the church and its parishioners had given them to help with replacing clothing lost in the fire.

Honey and Grits began barking excitedly as they waited for Lila to unlatch the gate, their tails wagging. "Okay, okay, hold your horses," she said, laughing softly.

"Patience has never been one of their virtues," Mama Tully said with a joyous smile.

The moment the gate opened, the pups

greeted Lila and then raced toward Mama Tully, loving her up, but with a more noticeable gentleness. From the moment she'd come home from the hospital, they'd seemed to sense she was in fragile health. The animals never pounced on her the way they did Lila and Finn, or even Mason, for that matter.

Lila hurried to change out of her church shoes and into her sandals to take the dogs out. "Ready?" she asked them as she headed for the front door.

Barking in response, the pups followed her out onto the porch. Lila prayed they would see to their needs and return without a chase. Sometimes they did, sometimes they didn't.

That thought had barely surfaced in her mind when both dogs took off toward the orchard. "Honey! Grits!"

"Let them go," Mama Tully said behind her as they disappeared into the orchard. "They'll come back. I'm sure they've just gone off looking for Finn."

Finn had gone to Mason's place after church, something their son had done the past two Sundays. Only today, he'd accepted their offer to stay longer than the hour or so he normally visited to join them for lunch. They'd been so patient, giving Finn time to acclimate to his new family without pushing him into any situation he wasn't ready for. Lila had no doubt he would enjoy taking part in lunch with the Landerses. She always had, could still remember all the happy chatter and playful teasing.

"I'll take a walk over there," Lila said. "I'd feel better if I knew for sure." Mama Tully's heart would be broken if anything happened to the dogs.

Mama Tully smiled knowingly. "Are you certain that's the only reason you're going to Mason's? To check on the dogs?"

Lila sighed. "Mama Tully, you have to stop hoping for something that will never be. It doesn't matter how I feel. I gave up any right to Mason's heart a long time ago. I can't force him to love me again, just because that's how I wish things were between us."

"There's a reason he's never gotten married," she pointed out.

Lila's heart stirred for the briefest moment before she tamped the unrealistic flicker of hope down. "Because he hasn't met the right woman yet."

Mama Tully quirked a thin brow. "Or maybe it's because the women he's met weren't you."

As much as she'd love to believe that was the case, Lila knew better. Mason's heart wasn't hers to hope for. She'd given that chance up a long time ago. But when Mama Tully had her mind set on something, there was no changing it. Redirecting the conversation was her only hope. "I really should get going. You wanted to start on those bows for Mrs. Landers, and I need to see where those little escape artists of yours have gotten off to."

Mama Tully could make the most beautiful wired ribbon bows, offering up her crafts every year for the annual peach festival Mason and his family held in front of their shop the second Saturday in August. The festival not only brought the community together but also helped raise money for the church's missionary program. Constance would put together raffle baskets, which Mama Tully's bows would decorate.

Mama Tully smiled at the mention of her beloved dogs and then nodded. "I do need to get started on those. The festival is going to be here before we know it."

"Not quite three weeks," Lila said with a nod.

"It's grown so much since you lived here. Wait until you see it."

"I won't be going," Lila replied with a frown.

"What do you mean, you won't be going?" Mama Tully practically gasped. "It's one of the biggest events this town has. And you used to love Constance's homemade peach cider."

She had loved Mason's momma's peach cider, and her pies, and her cookies—in fact, just about everything she made. "I don't think my going would be a good idea," Lila told her. "I don't want to make what should be a positive day for all negative. Jake and Violet would be uncomfortable with me there, and understandably so."

"Maybe by then they'll have come around," her foster mother said hopefully.

"Maybe so," Lila said with a smile, even though she felt nowhere near as confident as Mama Tully was in that ever happening. "See you in a bit."

"Don't hurry back on my account!" Mama Tully hollered after her. "I'll be resting comfortably in my chair making bows."

Lila waved in response, unable to keep the smile from her face. That came, not only from her foster mother's good intentions, but from being back in Sweet Springs. From finding the courage to make her way back to God and the forgiveness she'd finally been able to ask for. It felt as if through her return to the faith she'd walked away from so very long ago, through her return to God, the heavy weight of guilt that had been smothering her heart for so many years had finally begun to lift.

And after that morning's sermon Lila was even more grateful for the blessings she had in her life. Her early life might have been a heartbreaking struggle, but that hardship had led her to a better life. It had given her Mama Tully and the first real home she'd ever had. It had given her Addy, her best friend for life. It had given her Mason and taught her what real love was and, more recently, that those who genuinely seek forgiveness could find it. And it had given her Finn. It was true what they said: God is good.

Lila's gaze focused on the tree-lined path ahead as she walked along. She wondered how lunch with Mason's family had gone for Finn. Her son had been over to visit with Mason and his family several times, but this was the first meal he was sharing with them. Mason had wanted to ease their son into his life so as to not overwhelm him, something Lila was grateful for. She owed Mason so much. If not for his insistence that their son attend church while they were there, Lila wasn't sure they would have ever gone, even back home. Finn truly looked forward to going and was finally finding the faith she had never taught him—even as she was re-discovering it, too.

As she passed by what had been her and Mason's tree, Lila slowed, her thoughts drifting back to the past. To a time when she felt safe and happier than she'd ever been. To a time when she and Mason had talked and laughed and were the best of friends. When their love had blossomed right along with the trees that surrounded them. She had been so afraid to love him back at first. Afraid he would abandon her like her parents had. Over and over. And just when she'd finally come to accept the love he professed to her, feelings that went beyond close friendship, when she began to believe that they could have the future they had talked about having together, her parents' lives had been taken away. That day, that painful loss, had changed everything for her. But here she was, back in Sweet Springs, where she had been able to mend some long-broken fences, reconnect with her faith, and, while she and Mason couldn't be the family she longed for them to have been, her son finally has a father to look up to and a family who loves him dearly.

Barking erupted up ahead, in the direction of the Landerses' house, pulling Lila from those unwanted thoughts of her past.

She recognized those excited yips and yaps, and relief eased through her. Mama Tully had been right. The dogs hadn't run off elsewhere; they'd gone in search of Finn, maybe even Mason, of whom they were quite fond. Not that she could blame them. Mason just had a way about him, be it with rescued dogs or people. He was patient and kind and never failed to set one at ease.

"Pop-up!" Jake called out from somewhere behind the oversize two-story farmhouse.

"I got it!" she heard Finn exclaim.

More barking.

"Thatta boy!" Jake said, cheering Finn on. "Get ready for the next one."

Lila took in the happy chatter going on between Finn and his uncle as she stepped around the back of the house, grateful that the Lord had blessed her son with a family so willing to welcome him into its fold.

Her unexpected arrival took both Jake and Finn by surprise. The ball Jake had just tossed up into the air dropped down into the open glove Finn had extended high up above him and then rolled right back out as her son looked her way. The baseball hadn't even settled on the ground before Grits snatched it up.

"Momma," her son groaned as he watched the dog dart off with the ball.

"I didn't take it," she said defensively, but with a smile. "Grits did."

"He wouldn't have got it if you hadn't snuck up on us." He looked to Jake for confirmation of that statement.

Jake walked over to retrieve the ball from Grits and then turned to face Lila. "We weren't expecting you."

"I'm sure you weren't," she agreed. "I was out looking for Honey and Grits. They took off when I let them out to stretch their legs. Mama Tully thought they might be over here, and it appears she was right."

"I don't have to go home with you yet, do I?" Finn asked worriedly. "We just started playing catch."

"No," she replied, realizing that it would no longer be just her and Finn sharing the laughter and fun. He was now surrounded with those who brought him joy, in so many ways. She just prayed he would be able to get past the hurt she'd caused him, longed for the special bond they had once shared. The family that had recently spoken at church came to mind. They had been through so much, yet their faith had carried them through it all. Kept them strong. Like those wonderful people, she, too, would turn to the Lord for His guidance. Trust that He would bring about the emotional healing between her and Finn. With that in mind, she smiled. "You can stay. Just be sure not to wear out your welcome."

"Not a chance of that ever happening," Jake stated, flashing a grin at Finn. "He'll always be welcome here."

"I appreciate everything you and your family have done to make Finn feel welcome here," Lila replied.

He nodded and then looked to her son once again. "Finn, why don't you go see if Gramma Landers wouldn't mind fixing us a glass of lemonade?" His gaze shifted back to her. "Your momma, too, if she's not in a hurry to start back to your gramma Tully's."

Lila's eyes widened in surprise at the invitation. "I have time," she said, the unexpected turnabout in Jake's attitude toward her making her hopeful that they might be able to lessen some of the distance between them.

"Can we play more catch?" Finn asked his uncle.

"If there's time after we finish our lemonade," Jake replied.

With that, her son dropped the baseball glove he'd been using onto the ground and raced off toward the house. Honey and Grits, no longer interested in playing swipe the ball, chased after him, leaving Lila alone with Jake.

An uneasy silence fell between them.

"Where's Mason?"

"In the house," his brother replied. "He was out here taking turns tossing the ball to Finn with me but got a call about his upcoming mission trip."

"Oh," she said, biting at her bottom lip to keep from voicing her concern about the danger Mason was putting himself in going to the Congo. His decisions weren't any of her business.

"He shouldn't be much longer."

"That's all right," she told him as she clutched the pair of leashes in her hands. "I'm only here to get the dogs." *And to see how my son is faring*, she left unspoken. "I'll have my lemonade and then go."

"Now that you're here…" he mumbled, shifting uneasily where he stood.

Lila had known this day would come. "It's okay, Jake. Have your say."

"I intend to," he replied, but not harshly. There was more of a gentleness to his tone. "I was going to walk over to Mrs. Tully's later this afternoon to talk to you, but I think it would be best to do so now, while Finn's busy helping his gramma fix us some lemonade."

A knot of apprehension formed in the pit of her stomach. If she'd had any doubt that this was not going to be an exchange of pleasantries, Jake's need to make sure Finn wasn't around to overhear their conversation confirmed it. She owed it to Jake to hear him out, but before doing so, it was important to her to offer up another heartfelt apology. She needed to do so, because she had hurt him. Had hurt his entire family.

"Jake," she replied, "I know that nothing I say can ever make up for what I did to you and your family, but I truly am sorry for the choices I made back then."

"Lila—" he began, but she cut him off.

"You have every right to hate me," she admitted, unable to keep the words inside. "In my heart, I thought I was doing what was best for everyone involved. I thought wrong. I know that now." She hung her head, awaiting her due from Jake.

"Lila," he said more determinedly, "I don't hate you."

Her head snapped up, her gaze searching his. "You don't?"

He shook his head. "Don't get me wrong. I'm not happy with you for keeping Mason's son from him, from us, for all these years. The hurt that caused both then and now still cuts deep," he told her.

"I wish I could go back and change things," she said, shaking her head woefully.

"I do, too," he agreed with a sigh. "You know, Lila, I had begun to think of you as a sister, fully expecting you to become one through marriage to Mason someday, because I knew just how deeply my brother felt for you."

Her vision blurred with unshed tears. "I wanted nothing more."

"That's why your taking off the way you did didn't make sense to me," he admitted. "I'd known you'd had a rough life before coming to Sweet Springs, but I never stopped to consider back then that the things you'd gone through in your past might have stuck with you, altering the way you saw things, reacted to things. All I knew was that you'd come from an unstable home but had found a home here with Mrs. Tully that offered both love and support. And you'd found Mason. I couldn't understand why you would want to leave the life you had found here. Until last night."

Lila stood there, staring up at him. "Last night?" Then it hit her, and she stiffened. "What did Mason tell you?" The conversations she'd had with Mason back then and since her return had been between the two of them. It was a painful time that she didn't care to revisit any more than she had to. But then that had led her to turn away from the future she had dreamed of having with Mason. Maybe it was time to open up to his family about what she'd gone through, let go of the shame and the pain that she kept buried deep inside her.

"I didn't know how your parents died," he admitted. "Momma only said there was an accident, and Mason had never clarified what that had been. I'm glad he finally confided in me," Jake told her. "At least, where some things were concerned. Otherwise I wouldn't have understood as clearly as I do now your reasons for leaving. That beyond the shame you hoped to spare him, you didn't want him to feel trapped the way your daddy had."

A tear fell onto her cheek. The last thing she wanted to do was rehash her past.

"I'm so sorry, Lila," he said. "Sorry that you felt the need to run from the happiness you'd found here. Sorry that your momma and daddy couldn't get away from their addictions long enough to give you what every child deserves—a family who protects and loves them."

"And foolish me, I'd never stopped clinging to hope. I wanted my family to be a family."

"You wanted what every child wants," he said, his tone gentle. "I thought a lot about my talk with Mason last night, and when I woke this morning, I knew what I had to do. Finn deserves a family who surrounds him with love and the knowledge that he will always have a place with us. Any of us. Whether he's here or in Alabama. Not a family who is at odds with each other."

Jake stepped forward to wrap supportive arms around her. "We'll find a way to make this work, Lila."

"How?" she said with a sob. "We live in two different states."

"That's for you and Mason to decide. And it might not hurt to send a prayer heavenward for some guidance on the matter."

She would most definitely do that. Faith was a wondrous thing, as it seemed God had already begun answering her prayers.

Mason stepped from the house to find Lila wiping her eyes as she took a step back from his brother. A myriad of emotions filled him at seeing her distress. Protectiveness. Concern. The need to comfort her. Stepping off the porch, he strode toward his brother and Lila, a frown on his face.

"Jake," he growled, drawing both their gazes his way.

His brother held up a hand. "It's not what you think."

Mason looked to Lila and then back to his brother. "I think Lila's been crying after talking to you," he said, disappointment in his voice. "You said you were going to back off."

"Jake didn't make me cry," Lila said, surprisingly coming to his brother's defense. "Well, he did, but not in the way you're thinking."

Jake nodded. "I told Lila that we need to focus on Finn's best interest and act as the family we are to him."

"Your brother doesn't hate me," she said with a sniffle.

The tension in Mason slid away. He cast his brother a grateful smile. "Glad to hear that." Looking around, he asked, "Where's Finn?"

"Probably in the kitchen with Momma," Jake replied. "I sent him into the house to fetch some lemonade for us so I could have a few moments alone to talk to Lila."

"Jake tells me you opened up to him about my past," Lila said.

His good intentions appeared to be on the verge of stirring things up. "Jake, would you mind giving Lila and me a few moments alone to talk?"

His brother nodded. "I'll go see if Finn and Momma need any help pouring that lemonade."

When Jake had moved beyond hearing distance, Mason said, "He needed to understand."

"I told you things," she said. "Entrusted private pieces of my life to you."

"I know that," he replied. "And I held those confidences, even after you'd walked out of my life. But Jake needed to understand why you did what you did. Needed to let go of some of the anger he harbors toward you."

"Thank you," she said, surprising him. He had worried she might see what he'd done as a betrayal of her trust.

"We've got to do our best to pave a smooth road for our son to travel along as he grows into a man. That being said, we are Finn's family. You, me, Momma, Jake, Violet and Mrs. Tully."

"Addy, too," Lila reminded him.

A frown tugged at his lips. He was still not happy with Addy for keeping the truth from his family all these years. She and his momma had formed a close bond when she was living with Mrs. Tully, Addy spending hours helping Violet and his momma bake pies and other desserts to be sold at the market. Her silence had also felt like a betrayal, but if he were to practice what he preached to his brother about Lila, he needed to do the same with Addy.

"And Addy," he agreed with a nod.

"Mason…"

His gaze locked on those beseeching blue eyes. "Yeah?"

"Where do we go from here?"

He gave an honest shrug. "I'm not sure. This isn't a position I'd ever considered myself being in."

"Please don't take my son away." Tears welled in those troubled blue orbs, reaching a place in his heart that he'd forgotten existed. The part that had once loved her wanted nothing more than to make her happy.

But her happiness was no longer his responsibility. Finn's was. By all rights, he could go after at least partial custody of his son and have plenty of legal ground to stand on, all things considered. However, to do so would only cause more hurt, and there had been enough of that for all those involved to last a lifetime as far as he was concerned.

"Two wrongs won't make a right," he replied.

Her pretty features eased. "I wouldn't blame you if you did."

Same old Lila he remembered, always fearing the worst. "That's not how I was raised." Something his momma had reminded him of during one of their recent talks. And she was right. To be the man his momma would be proud of, the son his father had raised him to be, he had to do the right thing. Even if the right thing meant being apart from the son he'd only just discovered.

"There's so much we need to work out," she said with a sigh. "In a perfect world, our son would have two loving parents to share his days. But life doesn't always work out that way. I suppose all we can do is make certain Finn knows that he is loved and wanted by both his momma and daddy, no matter which of us he is living with at the time."

"Agreed," he said with a nod. "Finn tells me Addy might not be here now until summer's end."

She nodded. "It appears that way."

"Then we have time to figure it out." He walked over and picked up Finn's discarded ball and glove. "Now, how about we go inside and have a glass of lemonade with our son?"

Lila glanced toward the house. "I'm not so sure that's a good idea."

"I thought Jake agreed to put Finn first," Mason said.

"He did," she agreed. "But being cordial to me whenever Finn is around is one thing. To expect him, or your momma and Violet, to welcome me into their house is another."

"It's my house, too," he reminded her. They all still lived at home, working together to keep the orchard and the market thriving. Someday, probably not until they started families of their own, they would build places of their own on land their daddy had left them on the outer edges of the orchard. Until he and Lila had reconnected, there hadn't been any pull for him to live anywhere other than in the home he'd grown up in. Now those thoughts were stirring in his head, more often than not.

With a frown, she shook her head. "Thank you for the offer, but I can't stay." She glanced toward the house and then back to Mason. "Would you mind getting the dogs for me?"

"The dogs?"

"Honey and Grits," she explained. "They took it upon themselves to pay a visit to your place."

A grin tugged at one side of his mouth. "You mean they gave you the slip again."

She pointed a finger at him. "If anyone's to blame for their wayward behavior, it's you."

He chuckled. "Me?"

"Mama Tully said you had been spending time with them before she got sick, and then we both know you cared for them daily when she took ill," she said. "Therefore, any bad habits, along with their eagerness to buck authority, falls on your shoulders as far as I'm concerned." With a stubborn lift of her chin, she glanced away.

"Then I had better set aside a little extra time to work with them," Mason replied with a grin. "Can't have Mama Tully thinking that I corrupted her babies. I'd be happy to give you some tips on ways to keep Honey and Grits from getting bored. Because a bored dog is a dog guaranteed to get into mischief."

"That would be helpful," Lila said with a soft smile. "Because the truth is I have no experience whatsoever with pets of any kind."

"I kind of figured as much," Mason admitted with a grin.

"I really do need to get the dogs back to Mama Tully before she starts to worry over them."

"Why don't I go get Finn and the pups and I'll give you all a ride home?"

"I don't think Finn is going to appreciate his visit here being cut short because of me."

"We'll blame the dogs," he told her with a conspiratorial wink.

"Don't," she said.

Confusion filled him. "Don't what?"

"Be so nice to me," she replied. "It only makes me feel worse about what I did to you."

His expression grew serious. "I've got a son that I want very much to get to know, but my time to do so is limited. So any extra time I can squeeze out with my son, I'm going to grab onto."

"You can have all the time you need with him," she offered. "We'll be here all summer."

"And then what?" he said. "You'll be going back to Alabama and I'll be leaving for an extended trip to the Congo. It could be months before I get to see my son again."

"Can you reconsider?" she said.

"Everything's already set," he told her. "And there are only a few of us going on this mission trip. I can't short them a pair of hands when it comes to building that school. But I promise to pay Finn a visit the moment I return."

"In Alabama?"

"School will be in session," he reminded her. "I figure I will need to come to him once school's in, since harvesting time would be over. That is, once I get back from my mission trip." Or would that cause issues for Lila?

If she was seeing anyone, he was pretty certain they wouldn't be overjoyed to have Lila's ex and the father of her son show up. "Unless my coming there is going to be a problem for you. I could wait until Finn is on holiday break and bring him back here."

She shook her head. "Your coming to Alabama would never be a problem," she told him. "Finn would be thrilled to have you there. No doubt to show you off to all his friends."

"No relationship my being there might complicate?" he heard himself ask. A mental kick in the backside followed. He didn't want to go there. Didn't want to think about what Lila's personal life was like. It wasn't any of his business who she was seeing, or even if she was seeing anyone.

"No," she answered softly. "I'm not seeing anyone. And even if I were, I would make certain your being a part of our son's life wasn't an issue."

His heart gave a small lurch at her admission. "That's good to know."

"Mason," she said, almost nervously, "I know you and I will never be what we once were to each other, but I pray we can find a way to work with each other to figure out an agreeable plan for Finn's sake. That last thing

I want to do is put him through a long drawn-out custody battle."

He nodded. "We're on the same page there. This situation has been enough of a shock to him as it is."

She frowned. "He might not even want to stay with me after what I've done. It's all I can do to get him to speak to me."

"Would you like me to have a talk with him?"

"Nothing you can say to him will change the fact that I kept him from you for all these years," she replied. "I understand his resenting me for it. I just pray time will ease that hurt and he'll be able to find it in his heart to forgive me."

"I'll say a prayer for the two of you, then," he offered.

She looked up, meeting his gaze. "I would really appreciate that."

"Consider it done. Now, let's go have some lemonade and then get those little gadabouts home."

"There you are, my babies," Mrs. Tully greeted from her wicker rocker as Grits and Honey scampered up onto the porch to see her.

"They came to find me," Finn said with a smile as he raced behind them.

Mrs. Tully laughed. "I figured that's where they'd gone off to." Her gaze moved past Finn to Lila and Mason, who were bringing up the rear.

"Mason gave us a ride home," Lila explained.

"I see that," her foster mother said with a smile. "Thank you for delivering all my loved ones to me safe and sound. Would you like something to drink? I just made a fresh pitcher of sweet tea."

"We just had lemonade," Finn told her as he sat on the porch, prompting the dogs to hop all over him and douse him in eager puppy kisses.

"I see," she replied with a nod.

"How are you feeling?" Mason asked as he and Lila joined her on the porch.

"Better every day," she said, rocking slowly back and forth.

"Glad to hear it."

Lila crossed the porch and opened the screen door. "Be right back. I'm going to grab a handful of treats for Honey and Grits."

Mrs. Tully's eyebrows lifted. "You're going to reward these two for causing mischief?"

"Not exactly," Mason answered for her with a grin. "We're going to be using them to work on Lila's dog-training skills. They're a bit lacking."

"More than a bit," Lila admitted with a grin.

"There's some warm banana nut bread on the kitchen table," Mama Tully said.

"Banana nut bread!" Finn exclaimed, shooting to his feet. His excitement had the dogs dancing around and barking.

Mrs. Tully looked to Finn. "I've already sliced it, if you'd like to go get yourself a piece."

"Sure!" Finn wasted no time in scrambling for the door.

"Wash your hands first," Mrs. Tully called out.

"I will," Finn replied.

"I thought you wanted to learn how to care for Honey and Grits," Lila said as their son moved past her.

"Daddy can teach you and then you can teach me," he replied. Pausing at the door, he looked in Mason's direction. "You want a piece, too? I could bring you out one when I'm done."

"Maybe later," he replied. "After your momma and I are done working with the dogs. I'm afraid the smell of your gramma Tully's banana nut bread would be too much of a distraction for Honey and Grits."

"Okay," his son replied with a nod and then hurried into the house.

Shaking her head with a smile, Lila followed him inside to get the treats.

As the screen door swung shut behind them, Mrs. Tully laughed. "That boy of yours certainly likes his sweets."

Mason turned to face her.

"Reminds me of someone else I know," she went on.

Something else he and his son had in common. The thought of it warmed his heart. "He's got a lot of his mother in him, too," he replied honestly.

"The best of both of you," his neighbor pointed out.

"Momma says the same thing," he replied.

"Speaking of your momma, how did lunch go today with Finn and your family?"

"Better than expected," he answered. "Finn felt right at ease. To be honest, I was a little worried that he might feel uncomfortable without Lila there, but he did well. Violet adores him. And Jake is stepping right into the uncle role like he's been doing it for years."

"That makes my heart so happy," she said as she rocked back and forth. "Your momma and I have talked, and she tells me that Jake's been having a hard time dealing with everything that's happened."

Mason nodded. "I'd say that's a fair statement. But he and Lila had a chance to talk some things out today when she showed up looking for the dogs. I'm not sure Jake will ever completely forgive her, but he's agreed to set his anger toward her aside for Finn's sake."

"Praise the Lord," Mrs. Tully said, pressing a hand to her heart. "A prayer answered. And Violet?"

Mason propped himself up against a porch post. "We all need to try and set the past aside for Finn's sake. Even Violet. She's been keeping her anger inside, choosing to remain silent rather than start anything. I told her she needs to talk to Lila, let her know how she's feeling. Maybe even consider forgiving her, since her being Finn's momma will bring her into our lives often."

"Like you've done," she said with a soft smile. "I take it your helping Lila with Honey and Grits is merely you leading by example?"

"I suppose it is," he conceded. "But there's no denying Lila needs to know at least the basics to keep those two darlings of yours from running roughshod over her."

Mrs. Tully laughed softly. "They are a bit on the spoiled side, aren't they?"

"Let's just say they're well loved," Mason told her, his gaze drifting to the door.

"Not much has changed, I see."

He looked to Mrs. Tully. "I'm sorry?"

"You're still taken with that girl," she replied matter-of-factly.

Mason stiffened. "With Lila?"

"I'm not referring to Honey," she said. "And she's the only other *she* in that house. I've seen the way you still search her out whenever she's near."

"Don't let your imagination run too wild. I got over Lila a long time ago," he said with a frown. "The only reason she's in my life now is because of my son." Mason wondered if that last statement was directed more at himself or Mrs. Tully. And while Lila, as his son's mother, would inevitably be in his life, he knew better than to let his heart's guard down where she was concerned.

The screen door creaked slowly open, putting an immediate end to their conversation.

Lila stepped outside with what could only be described as a forced smile on her face. She clutched a sandwich bag filled with a colorful assortment of dog biscuits.

Mason tensed. Had she overheard him and Mrs. Tully discussing her? Heard a denial that wasn't exactly true? Because Lila's return to

Sweet Springs, and the feelings she stirred up inside him, had proved that he wasn't as over her as he'd once thought he was.

"I just realized how late it's getting," Lila said. "We can work with the dogs another time."

"It's barely midafternoon," Mrs. Tully pointed out.

"But Finn and I have taken up a good bit of Mason's workday," she explained. "I remember how much there is to do during harvest season."

Mason shook his head. "Not on Sundays. That's a day I set aside for spending time with my family and friends. And dog training," he added with a teasing grin, hoping to put a smile back onto her pretty face.

"I think it would be better if you saved your spare time for Finn," she replied, avoiding his gaze. "The two of you have a lot of catching up to do. I'll figure things out with Honey and Grits."

Guilt sliced through him. He had no doubt now that Lila had overheard what he'd said as she was returning to the porch with her bag of treats. That was why she was trying to back out of their plans. He hadn't set out to hurt Lila, but his carelessly spoken words had succeeded in doing just that. Now what?

Did he apologize? Or should he go, as she seemed determined for him to do?

"Oh, for goodness's sake," Mrs. Tully said from the rocker. "Mason wouldn't have offered to help you out if he didn't think he'd have the time. And you have to admit that learning a thing or two about caring for my rather *well-loved* babies couldn't hurt. They can be a bit on the troublesome side at times."

"I made the offer," Mason agreed.

Lila hesitated and then finally swung her gaze around to meet his. "If you're sure."

"I'm sure."

"Okay," she relented with a sigh. She held up the bag she'd brought out with her. "We have the treats. All we need now is the dogs."

"I'll get them," Mason announced as he made his way to the door. Opening it just wide enough for the dogs to slip through, he gave a short whistle. "Honey. Grits. Come."

The thumping of paws sounded across the hardwood floor inside. A second later, the dogs shot out through the open door. Grits first. Honey right on his tail. They moved to stand in front of him, looking up as if in anticipation of what they were about to be doing.

Grinning, Mason reached down to give both dogs an affectionate scratch behind their ears, feeding them words of praise that had their tails thumping against the porch floor. Straightening, he turned to Lila. "Ready?"

"Ready."

Mrs. Tully pushed up from the rocker, getting to her feet, much steadier than she had been when she'd first come home from the hospital. "I think I'll go in and have a piece of banana nut bread. That is, if my grandbaby hasn't eaten it all," she said teasingly.

"He might have," Lila replied with a smile, "if I hadn't told him to limit himself to one slice."

"One? Who eats only one slice of freshly baked banana nut bread?" Mason said, pretending to be aghast at the very thought of it. "Finn's a growing boy. He needs lots of food to fuel him."

"Healthy food," Lila said in a motherly tone.

"Banana bread is healthy," he countered. "It's made with bananas."

"And lots of sugar," Mrs. Tully said with a chuckle as she reached for the handle of the screen door. Glancing back over her shoulder, she said to Lila, "Seems to me you're not the only one who has some learning to do."

"Agreed," Lila said with a nod as the door closed behind Mrs. Tully.

Mason signaled for the dogs to follow as they made their way off the porch. "Maybe we can work out an arrangement," he said as they walked along.

Lila tilted her head to look his way. "What sort of arrangement?"

"You teach me some of the important things I need to know about parenting, and I'll teach you anything you want to know about caring for dogs."

"There shouldn't even have to be an exchange."

"True," he agreed, "but we can't change the past. And I need to know the ins and outs of parenting, at least the abbreviated version for now. Because God blessed me with the opportunity to get to know my son this summer before I leave on my mission trip. I don't want to mess things up."

"Like I did?" she said.

"I didn't mean to imply that," Mason said apologetically. "And while I don't have much experience with children, Momma tells me they are pretty resilient. Finn will get past this rough patch. And I'll do whatever I can to help the two of you work through this."

Lila lifted her gaze, looking up at him through misty eyes. "I don't deserve your kindness, and I know it. But thank you from the bottom of my heart. I'm willing to share whatever parenting information I can with you, whether or not you help me with Honey and Grits. Just know that I think your momma would be a far better source than me when it comes to some of those things. She's raised three wonderful children into three exceptionally giving adults. I, on the other hand, only had my time with Mama Tully to guide me in how I have been raising Finn. I learned it all by trial and error, doing the best I could."

"Despite the odds you had against you, being an unwed teenage mother and all, you've clearly raised our son well. You even succeeding in getting a college degree while caring for a baby."

"Thanks to Addy and her momma," she said. "And the childcare program my school offered its students. I knew that if I wanted more for my son than I'd had growing up, I needed a job that created stability. One that kept a roof over our heads and food on the table." And she had managed to do so. It hadn't been easy, but, unlike her own momma, she'd put her son's needs first. She wanted her child to grow up feeling safe and loved, and proud to call her his parent.

"I would have provided that for you," he said. "No matter the circumstances."

"I know that now," she said.

He stopped in the center of Mrs. Tully's backyard and turned to face her. "I intend to provide for my son from here on out."

She shook her head. "Mason, you don't have to. We're okay financially. It's enough that you want to be a part of our son's life."

"He's my child," he said. "Of course I want him in my life. From the moment I found out Finn was mine, there has never been any question in my mind about whether or not I want to be involved in his life. And I certainly intend to help support him."

"But this isn't something you planned for," she countered. "I don't want you to feel…" She hesitated, as if searching for the right word.

"Trapped?" he supplied, because he knew that was where her thoughts were. Not on him, or them, but on her past.

"Yes," she said, her reply sounding almost pained.

He released a heavy sigh. "Because it appears you need to hear this again, I'm going to tell you again, I am *not* your daddy, Lila. I have no intention of walking out of my son's life."

"No, Mason, you're not him," she agreed, meeting his gaze.

Honey let out a bark, jumping up at the bag dangling from Lila's hand at her side.

With a gasp, Lila tried to grab for the treat bag the impatient pup had just snatched from her grasp.

"Honey, no!" Mason commanded. "Drop," he said, his tone firm, and Honey immediately released the plastic baggie, letting it fall to the ground between her front paws.

"You are so good at that," Lila said, shaking her head in awe.

Mason bent to pick up the bag. "You've heard the saying 'been there, done that'? She's tried that trick on me before. Took me quite unexpectedly. Never let her short legs lull you into thinking she can't leap high when properly motivated."

Lila laughed. "I will be sure to store that tidbit of knowledge away for future reference."

Grits moved to stand in front of Mason, who now held the treat bag, and began barking loudly.

Honey wasted no time in adding her two cents' worth.

With a chuckle, Mason withdrew two dog biscuits from their plastic pouch. "We'd best get started teaching you a few things before these two decide to team up and abscond with these treats."

"Good idea," Lila agreed.

"We'll start with your teaching them to stay when you tell them to, and then to come when you give them permission."

"Sounds hard," she said, worrying her bottom lip.

"Not really," he told her. "It's more a matter of repetition, offering them a treat and praise when they follow your commands. Once they start to respond to you, we'll start taking the treats out of the mix and offering up praise only. Because you want them to listen to you whenever and wherever you might be, and there won't always be treats available to help with the coaxing."

Lila listened intently, taking in his advice on the basics of what it took to earn a dog's obedience. She asked questions and then told Mason she thought she was ready to give his teachings a try.

With a grin, Mason nodded. "They're all yours."

"Okay, kids," she said as she faced off with the tail-wagging pups, "I need you to sit."

"Be commanding," Mason told her, fighting a grin.

She glanced his way. "That was commanding."

"You're not inviting them over for tea," he said, his tone teasing. "You're letting them know who's in charge. Otherwise, you'll find yourself lying facedown in a rain-soaked garden again."

"Nothing like a reminder of one's very recent moment of humiliation to put things in perspective," she said with a smiling glance in his direction. "I am going to get the hang of this yet, Mason Landers. Just you wait and see."

And she would. Of that he had no doubt. Mason suddenly found himself wondering how he might slow her lessons down. Although he should be eager to finish up his offer to help her with Mrs. Tully's dogs, he found he was anything but.

Just as he once had, he felt content spending time with Lila now. Like his world was right again, which was so far from the reality of it all.

Chapter Seven

"This crop should be about ready to be harvested," Mason said, looking to his son as they walked through the orchard. It was the last week of July, meaning they were right on schedule. Jake and he would harvest this section within a few days, then finish up the season with the final crop during the first week of August.

"How can you tell?" Finn asked.

"Their color changes," Lila chimed in.

Mason looked her way in surprise. "You remembered that?" While they had spent more and more time together, mostly with Finn, occasionally without, they spent most of that time talking about their son, about Lila and Finn's life in Alabama, and about ways to make their situation work.

Lila smiled. "I remember a lot about my time here."

So did he.

"To all yellow?" their son pressed, clearly eager to know more.

It took Mason back to when he was a young boy, following his own daddy around the orchards every chance he got. He, too, had yearned to learn everything there was to know about the family orchards and the deliciously sweet fruits they produced. And now here he was, a generation later, standing in what had once been his father's shoes, sharing the knowledge he had gained over the years with his own son.

"Some," Mason replied, "but not all. Ripe peaches can also have a yellow-orange color to their skin. And it's not uncommon for the peaches to be lighter in color at the underside that faces the ground. Once the first crop is ready to harvest, we'll have workers come in to help handpicking the ripe peaches. Until then, your uncle Jake and I gather baskets of fruit that has ripened sooner than the rest and take them back to the house for your gramma Landers to cook with."

Stepping up to the nearest tree, Mason set a basket down onto the ground beside him and then reached up to curl his fingers gently around one of the dangling peaches. "You'll want to press a finger lightly into the fruit to test its ripeness before picking it." He did as he was instructing, his finger making a slight indent in the skin. "The outer part of the peach should give slightly, just as this one has." Glancing back at Finn, he said, "Give one a try."

His son looked a little panicked at the suggestion. "What if I squeeze too hard?"

"Then we'll have to eat it sooner," Lila assured him with a loving smile. "But I have faith that you'll do exactly as your daddy instructed. In fact, it'll probably come to you naturally. You're a Landers after all. Peaches are a part of who you are."

Finn looked her way, his expression falling. "But I'm not a Landers. My name is Gleeson."

Lila appeared dumbstruck by their son's reply, so Mason responded for her. "That doesn't make you any less of a Landers, son."

Lila, having finally collected herself, nodded in agreement. "My name isn't Tully, but that doesn't make Gramma Tully any less of a momma to me. But in your case there are things we can do to make you officially a Landers."

Mason's hand froze in place as he and Finn looked her way.

"I've been doing some research, and it's possible to add your daddy to your birth certificate and change your last name, if that's all right with him."

"We can?" Finn said, his face lighting up.

"I think that changing your name is something you need to think on awhile," Mason told him.

His son swung his gaze around his way. "You don't want me to have your name?"

Mason released the peach he'd been testing and stepped around the tree to where his son stood. Clasping a hand atop Finn's shoulder, he said, "I would love nothing more." He'd grown up wanting to have a big family like his own, hoping to have a son to carry on the family name, but after Lila left so did that part of his dreams. Now here she was, giving those back to him, and he was beyond excited at the possibility of that happening, but at what cost to her? "You've got your momma's feelings to think about," he heard himself saying, realizing that he didn't want to hurt Lila. If it meant letting that old dream go again, he would do it, because a difference in names didn't change the fact that Finn was his son.

"It's all right," Lila told him. "It's the name he should have had all along."

Finn turned to look up at Mason. "Can we change my name, Daddy? Please?"

Mason felt his heart expanding even more. Each day spent with his son—and admittedly with Lila, too—was giving that long-forgotten organ of his a reason to beat. "Your momma and I will set aside some time to discuss it." He glanced at Lila, who nodded in agreement.

With a whoop of joy, Finn threw his arms around Mason's waist, hugging him tight. "I can't wait to tell my friends my new name and that I have a daddy of my own, too, now."

Mason chuckled. "I look forward to meeting your friends."

Finn pulled away with a grin. "Wait until they see how tall you are. They won't be able to call me Pint once I grow as tall as you."

"Pint?" Mason repeated, quirking a brow.

"It's short for *Pint-Size*," Finn explained matter-of-factly. "That's what I'm called because I'm the smallest of us all."

"Doesn't seem like a very friend-like thing to do, if you ask me," Mason said.

"They all have nicknames," Lila explained. "Springer, who has a head full of red curls, Whistler, who has a small gap between his teeth and whistles whenever he talks, and

Sprinkles, whose cheeks are spattered with freckles."

"We got to pick our own nicknames," Finn explained.

The irritation he'd felt at first faded away. "I see."

"One of these days, I'll be able to change my name to Stretch, because I'm going to be tall like you!"

Mason glanced Lila's way to see her fretful expression. She knew, as Mason did, that Finn had inherited her smaller stature and was not likely to grow to be as tall as he was. But there was nothing wrong with that. "Maybe you will," he told his son. "And maybe you won't. What you need to keep in mind is that it's not height or the broadness of his shoulders that makes a man a man—it's his actions."

"I'm still going to keep drinking my milk," Finn replied.

Mason smiled down at him. "You do that. And be sure to eat all your vegetables, too."

His son made a pinched expression. "I'd rather stay pint-size than eat cauliflower or beets."

A deep chuckle erupted from Mason's throat. "You and me both." With that admission, he returned to the limb he'd been inspecting before their conversation had grown serious. "Now, let's find us some ripe peaches to take back to Gramma Landers. If they're on the firm side when you test their ripeness, leave them. That means they're not quite ripe yet. And when you pick them, be sure to lift the peach like this," he said, demonstrating with the one he'd tested earlier. Glancing back over his shoulder, he said, "Lila? We could use another pair of picking hands if you'd care to join us. Unless you've forgotten how," he teased.

"Picking peaches is like riding a bicycle," she said as she moved to join them. "Once you've done it, you never really forget how to do it again."

"Momma's picked peaches before?" Finn said in surprise as he rounded the tree.

"She sure has," Mason replied as he plucked the peach he'd been holding from its branch. "In fact, I remember her outpicking your uncle Jake and me more than once during harvest season."

Laughing softly, Lila reached up to check a peach. "Only because your brother helped me win."

Mason turned to her. "Helped you win?"

She kept her gaze fixed on the peach she was plucking from the branch in front of her.

"He might have given me some of his peaches when we were having our picking contests."

"Isn't that cheating?" Finn asked from the opposite side of the tree.

Mason looked to Lila, who met his gaze, and shook his head with a grin. "I'd say it was more your momma and Uncle Jake having some fun with me—on more than one occasion."

"Thank you," she mouthed, returning his smile. Then reached up to free another ripened peach from a limb above.

The fruit being just out of her reach, Mason stepped up next to Lila. "Here," he said, placing his larger hand over hers, "let me give you a hand." His much longer fingers assisted in giving the peach the additional nudge upward it needed to break it away from its limb.

Lila glanced up. "Thank you."

"Anytime," he said, letting his hand fall away. Then he promptly moved back to where he'd been standing, his heart remembering the times they'd gone out to pick peaches for his momma. Working together. Laughing together. Life had been so simple back then. "You doing okay over there, son?" he asked, trying to focus on something other than Lila and their shared past.

"I've got two peaches picked so far," Finn replied, bringing a proud smile to Mason's face.

It was such a surreal experience to be standing in his family's orchard, picking peaches with his son. His heart swelled with happiness. "Set them in the basket carefully and then gather up a couple more."

Finn did as instructed and before long he was depositing two more into the basket.

Mason gave a low whistle. "Look at you go. Keep that up and you're going to give your momma a run for the money when it comes to picking the most peaches."

"We're getting paid to do this?" Finn said, clearly not understanding the phrase Mason had chosen to praise his son's efforts with.

Lila's lips were lifted in an amused smile. Mason found his own grin hitching up even higher. "Maybe not with money, but I'm sure Gramma Landers will show you her appreciation for helping to harvest her some peaches by baking you something sugary sweet. Does that work for you?" he asked, peering at his son through the tree's fruit-laden branches.

"Yep," Finn said, his head bobbing up and down. "Gramma Landers makes the best sweets. Almost as good as Aunt Addy's."

"Your aunt Addy is a professional pastry chef," Lila reminded him. "She went to school to learn how to bake sweets. So I'm sure your gramma Landers would be honored to have her baking skills rank right up there with your aunt Addy's."

"She sure would." Mason carried a handful of peaches over to the basket on the ground, placing them gently onto the other ones. "Did you know that your aunt Addy first learned to bake desserts in Gramma Tully's kitchen?"

"She did?"

"Sure did," he confirmed. "She used to come over to visit and would end up helping your aunt Violet and Gramma Landers make baked goods to sell at our family's peach market."

"Which used to be a lot smaller than it is now," Lila told her son. "Your daddy and Uncle Jake have done a lot of work on the place, adding on to it so more people can come through during harvest season to buy baked goods and browse the market's gift section."

"Will I work there someday?" he asked.

God willing, Mason thought. Finn was a Landers, and the orchard and its busy market were family run. But if his son chose to focus his career sights elsewhere someday, he would support his decision. Thankfully, there were still quite a few years before Finn would have to make those choices. Until then,

Mason would teach him anything he wanted to know about the orchard, something he never grew tired of talking about when asked.

As the three of them worked to fill the basket, a comfortable silence fell between them. Mason's thoughts were centered on the time he had spent with Lila and their son in the weeks since learning that Finn was his. He'd gone from anger and resentment in the beginning to eagerly looking forward to the next time he'd get to see both Lila and Finn. Whether he was working with the dogs, helping them with Mrs. Tully's garden or playing catch, his heart had never felt so content. And now, in the orchard that was so much a part of who he was, harvesting peaches together, it felt like they were the family they should have always been.

His gaze drifted to Lila, who had fixed her focus on the peach she was lifting ever so carefully in her hand. This was the Lila he remembered. The Lila he had first fallen in love with. And there was no denying the truth that lay in his heart. He still loved her. Always would. But he also knew the time wasn't right to make his feelings known. He was going to be leaving the country at summer's end, and she was going to be going back to her life in Alabama. Trying to grow a relationship from the Congo would be nearly impossible. He had no choice but wait until he returned from his mission trip to see where things might go with Lila. He could only pray she would be willing to trust in his love for her.

Lila reached for another of Finn's T-shirts, still warm from the dryer, and began neatly folding it. Her thoughts were on the day before when she'd been picking peaches with Mason and Finn. The look on Mason's face when she'd said that she'd be willing to let Finn change his last name had nearly brought tears of joy to her eyes. It was a gift from her heart to both Mason and her son, both of whom she loved dearly.

"Lila," her foster mother said from the open doorway that led into the guest room Finn had been staying in.

Her gaze lifted from the basket of clean laundry she'd been folding. "Yes, Mama Tully?"

The older woman smiled. "You have a visitor in the living room. I'll be in my room if you need anything."

Before Lila could ask who it was, Mama Tully was gone.

Visitor? she thought to herself, wondering who it might be. Mason and Finn were working in the orchard that afternoon with Jake. So if not Mason or his brother, then who would be coming by to pay her a visit? Mrs. Landers, perhaps? But she was supposed to be baking that afternoon.

Not wanting to keep whoever it was waiting, she returned a still-warm pair of her son's jeans to the laundry basket and headed out of his bedroom to see who it might be.

Shocked couldn't even begin to describe Lila's reaction to stepping into the living room and finding Mason's sister sitting there, petting Honey and Grits, who were stretched out on each side of her on the sofa.

Violet looked up, offering a smile of all things, shocking Lila even more. "Hello," she greeted.

"Violet?" Lila said in bewilderment. "What are you doing here? Not that you're not welcome," she quickly amended. "I just never expected you to stop by to pay me a visit."

Violet had been the last holdout of the Landers clan. They saw each other at church on Sundays and occasionally when Lila came to get Finn after a visit with his daddy's family, but other than a brief exchange of niceties, they really hadn't spoken about what had happened.

"I was hoping we might talk," Violet said, sounding anxious.

"Sure," Lila said with a nod and then started around the coffee table, intending to take a seat on the unoccupied cushion at the opposite end of the sofa.

"Not here," Violet said, catching Lila before she sat down. "If that's all right with you."

"Okay," Lila said, taking a step back, her heart sinking. Things had been going so well. *Too* well. She should have known it wasn't meant to last. "We could step out onto the porch if you'd rather." It was probably better that way anyhow. She didn't want Mama Tully overhearing their conversation and getting upset because of it.

"I was hoping we could talk while we make a run into town."

Eyes widening in confusion, Lila said, "Excuse me?"

"I'm hoping you might ride into town with me. I'm on my way there to pick up some supplies for the baskets Momma and I are putting together for the peach festival's donation raffle," Mason's sister explained. "I know my brothers and Finn are out in the orchards harvesting and thought this might be a good opportunity for you and me to spend some time alone talking. That is, if you don't have any other plans for the next hour or two."

"No," Lila said, shaking her head. "I don't have any plans for this afternoon." Laundry could wait. This was far more important. She didn't want her son growing up with the tension that currently existed between her and Violet. Maybe once Mason's sister vented her feelings of disappointment and anger with Lila, some of that would ease. She prayed that would be the case.

"Then you'll go?" Violet replied, sounding almost as surprised as Lila felt.

The fact that Violet seemed eager for their talk did little to settle Lila's nerves, but she had to do this. Talking things over might not take away the hurt she'd caused Mason's sister through her actions. "I'd be happy to ride along." Turning down the invitation would be the cowardly thing to do. "Just give me a minute to grab my purse and let Mama Tully know where I'm going."

"I'll wait for you outside," Violet replied with a smile before letting herself out.

A smile. Odd, Lila thought as she left the living room and headed for her bedroom to get her purse. You would think if Violet was about to give her a comeuppance for what she had done to Mason and her entire family, a smile would be the last thing she'd be offering up.

Slinging her purse up over her shoulder, she made her way to Mama Tully's room. The door was open, so Lila stepped into the doorway. Her foster mother was seated in the overstuffed armchair next to the window, reading a book.

Her gaze lifted, meeting Lila's. Lowering the open book, she asked, "Is everything okay?"

"Violet asked me to accompany her into town to pick up supplies for the peach festival."

The corners of Mama Tully's mouth lifted in a buoyant grin. Clapping her hands together, she said, "I knew she would come around."

Frowning, Lila said, "Please don't get your hopes up too high. Violet said she wanted to talk in private, which is why she's invited me to ride along with her into town. That makes me believe she's ready to speak her mind about what I did to her family. Not that I didn't expect it to happen at some point."

"I suppose she might have a thing or two weighing on her heart that she wants to talk about." She searched Lila's face. "It might not be an easy conversation. Are you ready for it?"

"I have to be," she replied. "I was able to get past Jake's angry words and come out for the better. I pray this will be the same. Lord knows I deserve whatever it is Violet has to say to me."

"You're doing the right thing," Mama Tully said with a tender smile.

"I'm hoping to ease some of the emotional divide between Violet and myself, not only for my son's sake, but because she's Mason's sister, who—I'm sure you know—he adores."

"Very much so," Mama Tully agreed with a bob of her head. "And because she's his sister, Violet will find the same forgiveness in her heart that Mason and Jake have."

"How can you know that?" Lila asked skeptically.

"Because forgiveness is a part of the faith they've been raised on," her foster mother replied. "It's who they are."

Lila sighed, wishing her faith in that day's outcome was as strong as Mama Tully's. "I pray you're right."

"The Lord is always open for prayers," her foster mother said with a loving smile. "You might send one up to him before you leave."

"You can count on it."

"I'm so glad you've welcomed Him back into your life."

"So am I." So very glad. Doing so had given her an inner peace she never thought to have again. The comfort of knowing that no matter how bad things might get, He would always be there for her, helping her to get through those times. She'd been so hesitant to turn to prayer in the past, feeling unworthy when it came to asking God for anything. As she faced her past, worked at rebuilding relationships, she felt closer to the Lord than ever. More at ease turning to Him in prayer, trusting in Him to help guide her through the ups and downs that came in one's life.

"You'd best get going," her foster mother said, waving Lila from the room.

"I know." She didn't want to keep Violet waiting, but first there was something she needed to do. Stepping over to the chair Mama Tully was seated in, she bent to place a kiss on her foster mother's cheek. "I love you, Mama Tully."

"I love you, too, sweetie," the older woman replied, her voice catching with emotion. "Now, go and have a good talk with Violet."

Nodding, Lila headed outside where Mason's sister had said she would be waiting for her. Only the porch was empty. Lila wasn't sure if she should be relieved or disappointed, considering the mental preparation she'd done before coming outside.

A honk drew her gaze to the driveway, where Violet offered a quick wave through the open window.

Stepping down from the porch, she crossed the yard and rounded the front of the metallic-green Ford Escape. Taking a deep breath, Lila opened the passenger-side door and settled herself onto the sun-warmed leather seat. Pasting a brave smile on her face, she turned to Violet. "So," she said as she buckled her seat belt, "where are we headed to first?"

"Mrs. Benson's store," Violet replied as she shifted the car into Drive and pulled away from the house.

"The Flower Shack?" Lila said in surprise, memories of the past stirring in her mind. Mason surprising her with a bouquet. Mrs. Benson showing her how to make a bow so she could surprise Mama Tully with it on her birthday gift that year.

"Yes."

"Did someone else take it over?" After all, it had been years since Lila had lived there and, even then, Mrs. Benson had been past the age when most people chose to retire.

Violet laughed. "As if Mrs. Benson would

allow anyone else to make her flower arrangements."

"I can't believe she's still running the place. Mrs. Benson has to be at least—"

"Eighty-one," Violet finished for her. "And still going strong."

"I'm glad to hear it," Lila said. "Mrs. Benson was always so kind to me. But to still be seeing to that place on her own…" She shook her head in disbelief.

"Not all on her own," Mason's sister replied with what almost looked like a frown. "Braden helps her out when he's not at the station or out on a call."

Braden Benson had been one of Jake's closest friends. "So he followed in his daddy's footsteps and went into firefighting?"

She nodded. "As soon as he graduated high school, he went to the firefighting academy. He's been doing what he loves ever since."

"I'm sure his gramma appreciates the help."

"She does," she replied. "Unlike some he's come to the rescue of. But that's Braden, helping anyone and everyone in need."

Lila looked her way. "You say that like it's a bad thing."

"It can be," Violet answered. "But Braden's need to always be a hero isn't my business."

Lila got the feeling that they weren't talking about Braden's being a firefighter, but she wasn't about to delve any deeper. It wasn't any of her business. So she let the remark pass.

"You know," she said, looking Violet's way, "I have to admit that it seems so strange to see you sitting behind the wheel of a car."

Some of the tension seemed to ease from Violet's grasp on the steering wheel. "Why?" she asked, sparing a brief glance in Lila's direction. "I'm twenty-three years old."

"Because I remember you as that freckle-faced, pigtailed, thirteen-year-old girl you were when I…" She let her words trail off, wishing she hadn't brought up the past.

"When you ran away from Sweet Springs?" Violet supplied for her, her gaze fixed on the road ahead.

"Yes," Lila said softly.

"Well, it's been more than nine years since you left town," she said, glancing Lila's way. "You'll find that a lot has changed in that time."

"Violet," Lila said with a sigh of resignation, because there was no more dancing around the issue that lay between them, "is there somewhere we can go to talk before running your errands?"

She glanced in Lila's direction, her expression having grown serious, as well. "You must have read my mind. I was going to suggest we stop by the coffee shop first," she replied. "The outdoor patio should be fairly empty during this time of the afternoon."

Lila nodded, and an uneasy silence fell between them for the remainder of the drive into town.

Once they had arrived, Violet was the first to speak. "If you'll go grab us a table, I'll go inside and order us something to drink."

"I can do that," Lila said.

"Would you prefer coffee or tea? They have a large selection of teas to choose from."

"Tea would be fine. Thank you." Lila said as she stepped from the car.

"I'm having English breakfast. Would you like that or some other flavor?" Mason's sister asked as they met on the sidewalk in front of Poured with Love.

"English breakfast with honey," she answered, reaching into her purse.

"No," Violet said, covering Lila's hand with her own. "My treat."

One again, surprise filled Lila. "Thank you."

Violet let her hand fall away and then turned, making her way into the coffee shop.

Lila moved to the cozy little seating area that had been added sometime after she'd left

Sweet Springs. There were five small bistro tables, each with either two or four chairs placed around them. Unfortunately, the patio wasn't empty as Violet had hoped it might be. Two men in business suits she didn't recognize sat drinking coffee while their attention was focused on the laptop screen in front of them.

Once she was seated, Lila pulled out her cell phone, placing a quick call to Addy.

"Hello?"

"It's me," Lila said.

"Why are you whispering?" her foster sister asked.

"I'm sitting outside the coffee shop waiting for Violet," she answered.

"Mason's sister, Violet?"

"Yes," Lila confirmed. "She wanted to talk, so we came here. I'm waiting at a table out on the patio, but I'm not alone. There are a couple of businessmen seated a few tables away. Hopefully, out of hearing range, but I'm keeping my voice low anyway."

"She's meeting you there?"

"No, she drove me here. She's inside getting us tea."

"I'm so confused. Violet drove you there? I thought the two of you were on the outs."

"She came by Mama Tully's and asked me

to ride with her into town so we could talk away from her family and Finn and Mama Tully. I just wanted to give you a quick call to ask you to pray for us. I know this isn't going to be an easy conversation, but I hope it will be a start to setting things right between us. Not that I have any expectations of ever having the relationship with her I'd once hoped for."

"I will most definitely pray for you, Lila," her best friend replied.

"Would you mind praying with me?" Lila asked. "I know that's not something you do very often, so if you'd rather not…"

"I would be happy to," Addy replied without hesitation. "But I'll let you speak the words."

Lila tipped her head downward and closed her eyes. "Dear Lord, thank You for coming back into my life and for giving me the chance to right the wrongs that I've done. Please forgive Addy for her part in helping me and allow the Landerses to forgive her, too. And give me strength today as I sort through things with Violet. Amen."

"Amen," Addy joined in.

"To think I've been feeling so guilty about not being able to be there with you and Finn and Mama Tully. Maybe my work issues will prove to be a blessing. You and Mason have come to terms with the past and have been spending time together, something you might not have done if I were there."

Addy was probably right. She would have felt the need to split her time between all those she cared about.

"You and Violet will work things out," Addy said. "I have faith."

"I wish my faith in that happening was as strong as yours and Mama Tully's. But she and I weren't as close back when I lived here, because she was so much younger than the rest of us." Jake was only two years younger than her and Mason, whereas Violet had been four years younger.

"She's not a little girl anymore," Addy pointed out. "Violet and I have talked a lot on the phone over the years. Not nearly as much as Jake and I have, because he always seems to be closest to the phone whenever I call. But I can tell you that Violet has matured into a kind soul, always helping others, including her momma with the baked goods for their market. She even helps Mrs. Benson with her flower arrangement orders during the holidays and for funerals."

Violet hadn't mentioned helping Mrs. Benson at the Flower Shack, only that Braden helped his gramma whenever time allowed. But then Mason's sister probably wasn't eager to share her personal life with her.

"Well, Jake came around," Lila said with a note of hope in her voice. "Maybe Violet will be able to, as well."

"How is Jake?" Addy asked. "He picked up when I called to apologize to his family for my part in keeping Finn from them, but as soon as he knew it was me, he set the phone down and called for his momma to pick up."

"He took the news pretty hard at first."

"I've gathered as much. I was afraid Mrs. Landers might not give me the chance to apologize, either, but she did, letting me know she was hurt by my actions, but understood that my intentions were well-meaning. I am hoping that once I get there in person, Jake and I will be able to talk things out. His whole family, for that matter. Like you, I owe them all a heartfelt apology for my part in all of this."

"Addy," Lila said regretfully, "I'm so sorry your helping me has put you in a bad light with Mason's family. Especially Jake. I know how much you enjoyed your phone conversations with him." She prayed Jake would find it in his heart to forgive Addy like he'd chosen to forgive her. Maybe once Addy was finally able to take the time off to come see Mama

Tully she and Jake would have a chance to talk things out.

"He has a way of making me laugh when I really need it. I'm going to really miss that if he chooses to keep me shut out of his life permanently," Addy admitted.

"I'll do what I can to set things right for you," Lila told her.

"You have enough on your plate. I'll work on repairing my relationship with the Landers family once I get there. I will say this, I would do it all again, even knowing the cost I would have to pay for helping you out, because everyone deserves to have a safe haven in their time of need."

Lila immediately teared up. "I'll never forget what you did for me. For my son."

The door to the coffee shop swung open as Violet stepped outside, a lidded cup in each hand.

"I have to go," Lila told her in an urgent whisper and then ended the call.

Mason's sister made her way to the table Lila was seated at. "Sorry," she apologized as she held Lila's cup out to her, "Mrs. Filmore was working the counter today. And if you don't remember her from your time here, let me tell you, she's a sweet woman who loves nothing more than to catch up on all the go-ings-on in everyone's life."

"That's okay," Lila assured her as Violet settled into the chair across from her.

Violet looked so much like her brothers. Same dark brown eyes and dark, wavy hair. Smiling, she brought her cup to her lips, taking a careful sip.

When Violet said nothing more, just sat dipping her tea bag, Lila said, "I know you resent me for what I did to your brother."

Violet's gaze lifted.

"To your entire family, for that matter," Lila went on. "And I don't blame you one bit. Looking back as an adult, I see now that I had other options—none of them easy—but I didn't have to leave Sweet Springs."

"Why did you?" Violet asked. "Did you think Mason would cut you out of his life?"

Lila hesitated, trying to gather the words to explain.

"He loved you," Violet insisted. "I may have been a young girl at the time, but I was old enough to understand that my brother's heart had been broken by your leaving."

"I left Sweet Springs because I loved your brother with all my heart. If you believe nothing else, please believe that."

"You cared for him so much you ran away with his child, never to contact him again?"

"I know how it must look to you," Lila conceded, "but I truly believed that your brother wanted to become a preacher like your daddy had been. He talked so often about admiring what your daddy did, his devotion to the Lord and how he longed to serve the Lord, as well. I thought he was referring to someday preaching to his own congregation. I didn't realize it was the mission trips that he was referring to. So when I found out I was carrying his child, a child neither of us had planned for, a child created outside of the bonds of marriage, I knew that my staying here would put an end to his plans, to all his future dreams."

"Even if he had wanted to preach and that hadn't worked out because of the situation, Mason could have found new dreams."

"Nothing seemed that simple back then," Lila admitted, feeling tears grow in her eyes. "I was young and scared because of my own family history, and I knew what it would mean for your brother, for your family, if word got out that he had fathered a child out of wedlock. And you asked if I thought Mason might cut me out of his life because of the baby. To be honest, that was a fear I had in the back of my mind. So yes, that played a part in my decision to leave everything I loved behind."

Moisture filled Violet's eyes, too. "Oh, Lila. I'm so sorry you had to go through that. I can't imagine having to deal with such adult issues when I was seventeen. I was overwhelmed enough just trying to decide which dress to wear to my school dances."

"No, I'm sorry," Lila told her. "For keeping Finn away from the best thing that could have ever happened to him. For denying my son the family he's always wanted. For letting my past decide my future instead of trusting in the love of those around me and in the Lord."

"Thank you for saying that," Violet said with a soft sniffle. "I know you've spent some time at our house since you and Mason began working things out where Finn is concerned, but I felt like I had to keep up my guard for Mason's sake. Especially after Jake decided to give you a chance. Someone had to be looking out for my family so you couldn't hurt us again. But as I've watched you and Mason together, seen the change that's come over my brother since you came back into his life along with his son, I began to realize that your being back in Sweet Springs might be a blessing after all."

Lila, overcome with emotion, could barely

speak. Swiping a stray tear from her cheek, she managed, "Mason's been far kinder than I ever expected him to be."

"That's Mason for you," Violet said. "All heart. And very good at making others believe he's happy with his life. No matter how big a smile he's put on over the years, no matter how loudly he might laugh at times, I saw what others didn't. Knew what they didn't. That Mason's heart was forever broken after you left. Until you came back."

Lila felt her heartbeat quicken, but she said nothing. Didn't know how to respond. Because her heart was suddenly hopeful that Mason might not have stopped loving her completely. She'd certainly never stopped loving him. At the same time, her head cautioned her to tread carefully.

Violet went on. "I asked you to accompany me today to try and lessen the divide between us. Knowing now what I do, that Mason still cares for you, and I think you care for him—"

"I do." She did, even more so now than when they were younger, which she would have never thought possible. But they'd both grown up and could now better understand he'd stolen her heart all over again, even when it was already his to begin with.

"Then I'm hoping we can close that gap altogether. For Finn's sake as well as for Mason's."

Sniffling softly, Lila nodded. "I would like that very much. And I promise to earn back your trust, your entire family's trust. My son's, as well."

"Finn's like I was, Lila. Too young to truly understand the depth of it all."

"It's so hard," Lila groaned. "I don't want to burden him with the painful parts of my past, but there are some things he needs to know. Beyond that, all I can do is be the mother he deserves, loving him with all my heart as I await his forgiveness."

"He's a sweet boy," Violet said with a kind smile. "I'm sure his forgiveness will come soon."

"I hope so," Lila said. "I couldn't bear losing his love permanently."

"You won't," Violet said with conviction.

Lila sent her a grateful smile, praying Mason's sister was right.

"There's something else Momma and I wanted to ask you," Violet said. "Would you be interested in helping us with the peach festival like you used to?"

Shock didn't even come close to describing the way she felt at that moment. Shocked and blessed all at the same time. *Thank You,*

Lord, for this opportunity to not only set things right with Mason's sister, but to have a chance to be a part of something that once meant so much to me. Lila nodded. "I would like that very much."

"Finn, too," Mason's sister said with a smile. "If that's all right with you."

"I think he would enjoy that. Thank you for including us in something so special to your family."

"We all talked about including you in the festivity preparations and agreed it was the right thing to do," she explained with a smile. "Well, except for Mason."

Lila's smile sank. "He didn't want us to be included?"

Violet shook her head. "Oh no, that's not what I meant. We didn't tell Mason what our intentions were, just in case today didn't go as I had hoped it would. But it did, and now Finn will be a part of something his grandpa started years before, while supporting his daddy's upcoming mission trip to the Congo."

Anxiety stirred in the pit of Lila's stomach at the mention of Mason's plans. She had no right to ask Mason not to go, but she desperately wanted to.

"Lila?"

She blinked her troubled thoughts away and

forced a smile. "Just tell me what I need to do to help." She couldn't change Mason's journey, but she could help to make sure he had the funds needed to go into this mission trip fully prepared. And then pray that God would bring him back safely to her and their son.

"Can I have a pie?" Finn asked as he eyed the freshly baked, individual-serving peach pies cooling on the kitchen counter.

"Those are for the market bakeshop," Mason explained with a smile, remembering days gone by when he'd been the little boy standing at the kitchen counter.

His momma walked over and lifted one of the slightly warm pie tins from the counter and then grabbed a fork from the drawer. "I don't think anyone's going to notice one little pie missing from the bakery display case," she said, setting it down on the kitchen table. Then, turning to Finn, she held the fork out to him and inclined her head toward the lone pie resting atop the checkered tablecloth. "It's all yours."

With a squeal, Finn dropped into the kitchen chair. "Thanks, Gramma!" he said, digging his fork right in.

"I guess they won't miss two, either, then," Mason said with a grin as he helped himself to another of the cooling pies, grabbed a fork and then settled himself across from his son, whose sun-tinged cheeks were already filled with a forkful of peach pie. So this was how his own daddy had felt, sharing the fruits of his labor with his children. In Mason's case, his son. The first of the next generation of Landerses.

"Make that three," Jake chimed in as he crossed the kitchen and grabbed a pie for himself.

With a sigh, Constance grabbed two more forks from the kitchen drawer and then picked up a pie. "Might as well make this a family thing." She handed one of the eating utensils to Jake and then joined them all at the table.

Lila and Violet found them when they stepped into the kitchen moments later.

"Momma," his sister gasped, "are those the pies we made this morning for the market bakery?"

"Maybe," their mother muttered past a mouthful of pie and a grin.

"They're really good, Gramma," Finn said between chews. "I bet you'll sell lots of them."

"Not from this batch," Violet said as she scooped up one of the remaining pies and took her seat at the table. "There's almost none left to sell." Reaching out, she snatched

Jake's fork out of his hand. "You're done, so you won't be needing this any longer."

"I'm glad you like them," his momma said, laughing happily.

It was the first real laughter Mason had heard from her since his daddy died. Hearing it made his heart incredibly happy.

"I'll make another batch tonight," she told them, apparently not the least bit ruffled by the thought.

"I'll help you, Momma," Violet volunteered.

"Thank you, honey," their momma replied. "Now, Lila, grab yourself a fork and a pie and come join us."

"I don't want to intrude," she replied. "I just came in to see if Finn was ready to go home yet."

"Not yet," her son replied without hesitation as he feasted on his pie.

"You're not intruding," his mother assured Lila, telling Mason that his family, at least two-thirds of it, had finally forgiven Lila and was now welcoming her to be a part of their lives. Violet, he had faith, would come around, as well. Their acceptance of Lila meant more than they could ever know, considering the ever-deepening feelings he had for her. "Now, come and join us."

Lila grabbed herself a fork before picking up one of the few remaining mini pies from the counter.

"Sit here," Jake said, freeing up the chair closest to Mason as he moved to one of the vacant chairs at the other end of the kitchen table.

His momma turned to Violet. "How was your trip into town? Were you girls able to pick up everything I needed?"

It was only at that moment that it settled into Mason's thoughts that his sister had just arrived *with* Lila, not at the same time as her. He immediately stopped chewing the forkful of pie, his gaze shifting from his sister to Lila and back again. How had he missed such a momentous happening when it had been right there before his eyes?

"Wait a minute," he mumbled, forcing down the bite of pie he'd been enjoying. "The two of you drove into town together?" Prayers did come true.

"Not only did we drive into town together," his sister said with a smile, "Lila and I had tea at Poured with Love and then did some shopping for Momma."

Mason was tempted to ask Jake to pinch him, certain that this had to be a dream, but he recognized the sweet, subtle scent of vanilla that filled the air around him: the perfume Lila always wore. Dreams didn't come with smells, as far as he knew, so this moment was actually happening.

"How..." he began. "What I mean is—"

"*We* are Finn's family," Violet explained. "It was time that Lila and I talked things out, which we did today."

He looked to Lila, taking in her relaxed smile, and his heart warmed. "Glad to hear it."

"You're not mad at Momma anymore?" Finn asked with a frown.

Violet shook her head. "I'm trying to move past my anger."

"Why?" he asked in genuine confusion.

"Because offering forgiveness is the Christian thing to do," his sister told Finn and then looked to Lila. "Especially when the person being forgiven recognizes what they've done to cause the hurt and is genuinely seeking to make amends for it." Shifting her focus back to Finn, she went on, "Your grandpa Landers taught us that from the time we were young children, sharing that same message over the years during many of his Sunday sermons."

"Grandpa Landers was a preacher?"

"For most of his life," Mason answered.

Finn took a moment to take that information in before looking beseechingly to his aunt Violet. "But what if you're too mad to take someone's *I'm sorry*?"

Mason saw the hurt those words caused Lila as she struggled to blink back tears. He wanted to reach out, to cover her hand with his own and give it a gentle squeeze of reassurance. But he held back.

"Anger can be a heavy weight on one's heart," his momma said, her tone gentle. It was a subject she and Mason had discussed in depth after he'd learned that Finn was his son.

"We've all made mistakes or have done things we regret," Mason told his son. "You, too, I'd venture to guess."

Finn pressed his lips together. Then he looked to Lila before lowering his gaze to the table. "I asked God to take me away from you and let me live with my daddy."

Lila gasped, bringing a shaking hand to her mouth.

Their son looked up at her, regret in his eyes. "But I didn't really mean it. I just don't want to live so far away from my daddy and Gramma Landers and Gramma Tully and Aunt Violet and Uncle Jake and Grits and Honey."

Mason watched as Lila turned to gather Finn in a loving hug. A surge of emotion swelled in his chest as their son, instead of pulling away as he had been doing, accepted and returned his mother's embrace.

"We'll find a way to make things work," Lila told Finn. "Maybe I can find a job teaching closer to Sweet Springs."

Their son's face lit up with pure joy at that possibility. "You mean it, Momma?"

A sheen of unshed tears blurred Mason's vision as he watched the emotional exchange between the two. The moment touched his heart. His son finally was moving toward forgiveness where his momma was concerned. His entire family had accepted Finn and, eventually, Lila. And then to hear that there was a possibility of Lila and their son moving to Georgia, maybe even to Sweet Springs itself. He wanted them near, wanted to make that dream he and Lila had once shared—of having a future together—a reality. Wanted it more and more with each passing day.

"Yes," Mason heard Lila say as he fought to control the onslaught of emotions he felt at that moment. "Coming back to Sweet Springs has been one of the hardest things I've ever had to do," she told their son. "Having to face my past. Admitting a truth I'd been holding inside for so long. Seeking forgiveness. But returning to Sweet Springs after all these years has also helped me to heal emotionally, to reconnect with the Lord, and has reminded me what true heart's contentment really is." She looked to Mason, smiling tenderly.

He returned her smile, understanding completely what she was referring to. With Lila back in his life, in his heart, and a son who was a living reminder of the love between them, he, too, knew the true meaning of a heart's contentment. Looking down at Finn with a tender smile, she said, "I want you to know that same kind of happiness."

"I have a daddy now," Finn replied and then glanced around the table at the smiling faces staring back at him, "and a whole new family. That makes me really happy."

"Me, too, son," Mason said, his voice husky with emotion.

"Us, too," his momma joined in, bringing about nods of agreement from Violet and Jake.

Lila looked his way, and her smile softened even more. Mason knew at that moment that he would do whatever it took to keep Lila, the woman he loved, in his life. He made a silent vow at that moment to bring his family together for good as soon as he returned from his mission trip, because every day spent without them was one day too many.

Chapter Eight

"Here's the last of the dance floor," Jake said as he lowered the remaining sheets of foam-backed plywood onto the ground next to Mason.

Mason sat back on his heels and dragged a rolled-up sleeve across his brow. He and Jake had finished up the harvesting a few days earlier, a little sooner than anticipated. That gave them a little more breathing room when it came to getting things set up for the peach festival that coming weekend. "I'll get those hinged together with the rest and then we'll be ready to put the vinyl flooring over it." Though his family always hosted the peach festival, they had finally gotten smart this year and figured out a way to build an outdoor dance floor that could be disassembled and stored away.

"I'll go grab the flooring," his brother said and then strode off around to the back of the main house to the pole barn they'd erected five years before to store festival supplies.

Grabbing the top sheet of the remaining dance floor pieces, Mason settled it into place and then reached for a hinge to attach it to the portion he'd already put together. Then he grabbed his cordless drill and a handful of screws to secure the hinge to the plywood.

"Tired of mowing this big old front yard so you've decided to cover the entire yard in plywood?"

Grinning, Mason stopped what he was doing and glanced back over his shoulder to find Lila standing there. "Never thought about it," he admitted. "But that would allow me to spend more time doing other things, like taking long walks with you through the orchard."

"That would be nice," she said with a smile.

Their conversations had grown more and more comfortable over the months she'd spent there that summer, so like those they'd once shared back when they were young and falling in love. With each passing day, they had moved further away from the pain and heartache of their past and closer to the rightness he remembered. And now it just felt right.

Lila was the only woman his heart had ever yearned for. The only woman he'd ever imagined being his wife.

Setting his drill down, he stood and turned to face her, grin still intact. "I'm afraid I'm going to have to wait to start on that project until after the festival." Inclining his head toward the pieced-together plywood behind him, he said, "I've got a dance floor to build so that I can request a dance with you at the festival this weekend."

"An actual dance floor?" she said, eyeing the project admiringly.

"A temporary one," he replied, "but yes."

"I remember kicking off our shoes and dancing barefoot in the grass for hours."

He chuckled. "It didn't take a peach festival to have you running around shoeless. You were barefoot more often than not when we were growing up."

She lifted her sandaled foot and wiggled her toes. "I've grown up since then."

Yes, she had. Into a beautiful, strong, independent woman. Into a loving, caring mother. Into the woman he intended to marry. "You're more than welcome to give in to your inner child and dance barefoot on this dance floor next weekend."

"I'll keep that in mind," she replied. "But it won't be the same."

"Agreed," he said. "However, we learned our lesson a few years ago when it rained for several days before the festival. The ground was a mess, forcing us to cancel the dancing portion of the festivities. Jake and I knew we had to come up with something to keep that from happening again."

"I think it's a great idea," Lila remarked, her gaze sliding to the pieces of joined plywood. "Far less chance of someone twisting an ankle on a level dance floor."

He nodded.

Lila glanced in the direction of the market and then back to Mason. "I'd offer stick around and lend you a hand, but I promised your momma and Violet that I would stop by today and help them get the market goods ready for this weekend's festivities. Mama Tully will be over in an hour or so. She was finishing up some bows your momma wanted for the porch posts in front of the market."

"I'm sure they're appreciative of your help," Mason told her. "Both you and Mrs. Tully. Things tend to get a bit hectic around here the week of the festival."

"I remember," she said softly. "For the first time ever, I find myself not looking forward to the start of school. The end of August will mean going home and leaving all of this behind. I suppose I should be grateful that Addy hasn't been able to get the time off yet to come here. It's given me the time needed to right so many wrongs and to realize the true extent of what I'd given up."

He nodded in understanding. "I'm grateful for the chance we've been given, too."

"I'm going to miss you and everything about Sweet Springs so much. The people. The church. Your family and Mama Tully." She lifted her gaze to meet his. "But most especially, you."

"Maybe you should consider moving back," Mason suggested, trying not to push her too hard, but wanting to put that option out there. Wanting to let her know that she'd be welcomed there for longer. "Look for a teaching job around here like you mentioned to Finn."

"You have no idea how tempted I am to give it a shot," she replied.

He couldn't keep the smile from his face. "Something tells me Finn wouldn't be too adverse to your moving here." Mason glanced around. "Speaking of our son, where is he off to?"

"He headed straight for the market as soon as we stepped out of the orchard. Your sister called earlier to tell him your momma had just made some peach and caramel-glazed coffee cakes and needed a taste tester."

Mason glanced in the direction of the market and shook his head with an exaggerated sigh. "Looks like I've not only been replaced as Momma's taste tester, I've moved down a notch on my son's favorites list. Momma's baking edged me out."

Lila laughed and reached out to place a soothing hand on his forearm. "Don't worry, Mason. You're still at the top of my favorites list, along with our son, of course."

His gaze locked with hers, his expression growing serious. He loved Lila so much. It was hard keeping those feelings inside. But he had wanted to give her time to figure out her own feelings toward him. He felt her heart opening up to him as his was to her, but neither of them had expressed those emotions verbally yet. "And you're at the top of mine," he said. "Right alongside Finn."

They stood staring into each other's eyes for a long moment. Then Mason lowered his head in a tender kiss.

Lila returned the kiss, her response confirming everything he already felt.

When the kiss ended, he looked down into her beautiful blue eyes. "I love you, Lila Gleeson."

"I love you, too, Mason. I've never stopped loving you."

His heart swelled. "Wait for me. When I get back from my mission trip, I want us to give our relationship another chance. Because when I think of my future, it's you I see there."

Tears shimmered in her eyes. Nodding, she said, "I want that, too. I'll wait however long it takes. Just promise me you'll stay safe over there. I couldn't bear it if anything bad happened to you."

"I will do what I can on my end," he promised. "But my life's course is in the Lord's hands."

"Then I'll pray for you every day," she told him. "Because I want us to be the family we always should have been."

It already felt like they were a family whenever he and Lila and their son were together. But he wanted more. He wanted forever with Lila. A house filled with children. A lifetime of deep faith and shared smiles.

Someone cleared their throat, and Mason and Lila took a step back from one another.

"I hate to interrupt," his brother said, "but this roll of vinyl flooring is getting a little heavy."

Mason chuckled. "Jake's giving me a hand

with the construction of the festival dance floor."

"I should be getting to the market anyway," Lila said. "Your momma will be wondering where I am."

"Oh, I think they'll know," Jake said with a grin as he lowered his load to the ground next to the nearly constructed dance floor.

"I'll walk you and Finn home later," Mason told her as he moved back to the piece of plywood he'd been working on when she'd arrived.

"I'd like that," she said. "Bye, Jake."

"Bye, Lila."

Mason stood watching her leave. There had been so much more he'd wanted to say to her, but his brother's untimely arrival had forced Mason to hold back. But they would talk, and he would make certain Lila had no doubt as to how committed he was to making their relationship work.

Halfway across the yard, Lila stopped to remove her sandals. Dangling them over the back of her shoulder, she looked back and flashed him a playful grin before continuing on her way, walking barefoot through the grass.

Mason couldn't keep the smile from his face.

"If you aren't a man in love, I don't know who is."

He turned to his brother. "She's always had my heart." Even after she had broken it.

"Not the best time to be leaving for the Congo," his brother muttered as he set to work.

"Don't remind me," Mason replied with a frown. "It's the first mission trip I've ever regretted signing up for. And not because the Congo is a riskier place than most. It's just too soon. I've only just found my son."

"You've only just reconnected with your one true love," Jake added with an understanding nod.

"That, too," Mason said with a sigh. "I told Lila that I love her and want to give our relationship another try. Not only for our son's sake, but because I know in my heart that I would regret letting past hurts keep me from seeing if we can make it work this time around."

Jake didn't appear the least bit surprised. "How did she react to that?"

Mason's smile hitched higher. "She told me she loves me, too." He looked to his little brother. "I want to be with her. Want to make her and Finn my family. I just pray my stay in the Congo passes by quickly so I can make that happen."

"You deserve to be happy," Jake said, emotion pulling at his words. "You've always given your all to our family. Even more so after Daddy died. When Violet and I could barely function because of our grief, you stepped in to be the man of the family, taking over the running of the orchard, shouldering all our burdens in the weeks and months after. I don't know how I can ever make that up to you. All I can do is let you know that I thank the Lord quite often for giving me you as my big brother."

Mason met his gaze. "I did what I did because I love you and Violet and Momma."

"Love you, too," his brother said.

"I want what Momma and Daddy had together, and I know I can have that with Lila. It's there. It's always been there."

"Daddy!"

Both men turned to look as Finn raced toward them, a wide grin on his face.

"Whoa," Jake said, holding up a hand in a gesture for Finn to slow down, which he did. "There are a lot of tools lying around you could trip on if you're not careful."

Finn glanced around and then looked to Mason. "Gramma Tully said to hurry before Grits eats Momma's shoe."

Eyebrows went up. "Her shoe?" Jake questioned.

Mason recalled Lila's playful gesture as

she was leaving and grinned. "Your momma needs to start keeping her shoes on her feet." He looked to Jake. "It seems I'm needed."

Jake chuckled. "So it does. Go rescue Lila's shoe. I've got this," he said, motioning toward the nearly completed dance floor.

"Thanks." Mason turned to Finn. "Let's go." With that, father and son broke into a fast jog in the direction of the market.

That week had flown by, everyone busy with last-minute preparations for the peach festival. And now here it was. Crowds were milling about the yard, playing games and buying raffle tickets on the baskets Lila and Violet had collected. Inside the market, people were supporting the cause by buying baked goods and specialty items. Baskets of freshly picked peaches were flying out the door.

Mason couldn't help but think about his daddy, knowing in his heart that he would be proud of how they'd been able to grow their annual mission trip fund-raiser.

"Do you have a moment?" Jake asked, inclining his head in the direction of the house.

"Can it wait?" Mason asked. "I've got to bring more peaches up to the market. We ran out already."

"This won't take long, but it's something I'd rather discuss in private."

His brother sounded serious. Mason's brows drew together in worry. "Sure. Let's go."

They crossed the yard, away from the festivities taking place in front of the family market onto the porch of their house.

Jake turned to face him. "I wanted you to hear this from me first."

"Hear what?" Mason asked.

"That I asked to take your place on the mission trip to the Congo."

Mason shook his head, trying to process what his brother had just told him. Especially since it had come from out of the blue. "Wait a minute. What are you talking about?"

"I went to talk to Reverend Hutchins a couple of weeks ago to ask if there would be any issues with my taking your place if you should decide to back out for personal reasons. He looked into it and said that because I'm already a part of their missionary program, have all the travel paperwork I would need and am up-to-date with all the necessary vaccinations, it could be done. All I would have to do is secure my own airfare since your flight reservation can't be transferred over to me."

"Jake," Mason groaned, gratitude causing

his voice to crack. What his brother was offering to do for him went above and beyond the everyday things brothers did for each other. He'd like to think he would have made the same offer to Jake if the tables were turned. "What are you thinking?" he forced out. "The Congo trip is going to be several months long. Not to mention some of the safety concerns that exist there."

"I'm well aware of the conditions and the risks involved in this mission trip. But my nephew needs his father here in the States with him so that the two of you can continue building your father-son bond," his brother replied. "Then there's Lila. You two are starting over, and your relationship doesn't deserve to be put on hold. You're so close to having that family you always wanted with her."

Mason swallowed hard. What his brother was offering… Emotion clogged his throat, forcing him to clear it. "I can't ask this of you."

"You didn't," his brother said. "It's something I want to do. I have no relationship ties to hold me back. And I can wield a hammer every bit as good as you, big brother. Let me go help build that school while you stay here and build your family."

"I'm going to ask her to marry me," Mason said, something he'd been wanting to do but had decided it better to do after he'd returned from his mission trip. His brother's selfless offer changed everything.

"You have my blessing," Jake told him, not appearing the least bit surprised by Mason's announcement. "In fact, I'm pretty sure you have our entire family's approval. We've all seen the love that exists between you and Lila. And it would make things a lot less complicated where Finn is concerned. No need for him to bounce back and forth between homes. He'd have one with both of you in it."

Mason frowned. "One big hitch in my plan. I don't have a home of my own."

"We've all got acreage Daddy left us in his will to build on. So start building. It's not as if we don't have room to accommodate two more in our big old farmhouse while that's being done."

"You make it sound so simple." But he would have to make some big decisions before those things could happen. Lila had already talked about moving closer, but was she ready to leave her job in Alabama and move back to Sweet Springs? He had no doubt she could find another teaching position in the area. Maybe not for that coming year, but she could always substitute until something opened up. But none of that would even come into play if Lila wasn't at a place where she was ready to accept his offer of marriage.

"It is. God brought Lila into your life for a reason—twice," Jake pointed out. "I'd say that's a pretty good sign that the two of you are meant to be together." Over in front of the market, music began to play, signaling the start of that afternoon's dancing. "Speaking of being together, I believe you promised Lila a dance. You'd best get going."

Stepping forward, Mason pulled his brother into a bear hug. "Thank you, Jake. You're the best brother and friend a man could ever hope for. God be with you when you take my place in the Congo."

His brother clapped him on the back as he returned the hug. "He always is."

"I was starting to panic, as usual, but everything really came together."

Lila looked to Violet, who was smiling happily as she took in the goings-on around them. She had done a lot to make sure the her family's peach festival fund-raiser would go off without a hitch. Her organizational skills were beyond impressive.

"It certainly has," Lila agreed.

"We're bound to run out of everything," Violet said happily. "Hopefully Mason gets back with those peaches soon. People are waiting for them."

And they were, waiting in a circle around the empty peach display, plastic shopping baskets in hand. "I don't remember there being this many people in attendance back when I used to come help with your family's peach festival."

"It's grown a little bigger each year," Violet said. "But most of that growth came after Mason and Jake added on to the market and expanded our orchards. People started coming in from surrounding counties to shop at the market and from that found out about the festival. The increased attendance has been such a blessing for our church. The more festival attendees we have, the more money we are likely to bring in for the missionary program. Which, this year, of course, happens to be Mason's mission trip to the Congo."

Lila's already anxious stomach knotted up even more at the mention of Mason's upcoming journey. As his departure day drew near, she couldn't help but think about the time they would be apart, separated by distance and with little contact, as Mason would be busy trying to get that school built as quickly as possible. She prayed that he and his fellow missionaries would be able to accomplish what they were there for without any issues and that Mason would return home safely.

"Lila? Are you okay?"

She blinked and then shifted her focus back to Violet. "Sorry. I'm just a little over-whelmed by everything." While she couldn't be more supportive, or proud, of his com-mitment to the Lord and helping others, she couldn't help but dread the thought of saying goodbye to Mason and heading back to Ala-bama, where it would just be her and Finn. Her time back in Sweet Springs had reminded Lila of what the word *home* really stood for. It was a place where one felt safe, felt peace and contentment, and was surrounded by people you cared about and who truly cared about you. It was a place where people, through the love of God, forgave and accepted. And, to her, *home* was Mason. She would do what-ever it took to be with Mason. To finally have the dream she'd long ago denied herself. Be-cause she and Mason and Finn were that fam-ily she'd always longed for.

"You'll get used to it," Mason's sister as-sured her with a smile. "Give it a year or two."

Lila's eyes teared up with Violet's words. Mason's sister spoke as if Lila was already a part of their future. That touched her heart, knowing she had truly been accepted back into Mason's family fold.

"I don't mean to interrupt," a familiar voice said behind Lila.

"Not at all." Violet's smile widened. "She's all yours."

"That's my hope," Mason replied.

Lila's heart skipped a beat. She turned, her gaze lifting. Mason stood smiling down at her as if she were the only person there instead one of a couple hundred.

"The dancing has started," he said. "I was hoping to get you out on the floor with me as soon as I reload the peach display." He inclined his head to the crates he'd brought in with him.

"I'd love to, but..." Lila let her gaze sweep the inside of the busy market, where people were carrying baskets. "We're so busy. I wouldn't want to leave Violet, your momma and Mama Tully to handle all this on their own."

"I think we can manage," Violet assured her, gently giving Lila a nudge. "And we have additional hired help working today. Now, go dance with my brother while I relieve Mrs. Tully at the register." She walked away, leaving Lila there with Mason.

"I'll help you with those peaches," she offered. They filled the tiered stand and then headed outside to where the dance floor was already filling up with festival goers. Around them, people feasted on food offered by an assortment of local vendors, who'd paid a set donation fee to be able to have a table at the festival. Others perused tables filled with homemade crafts and jewelry. Children ran around, pastries in hand, playing various games that had been set up throughout the festival.

Lila smiled as she caught sight of Finn running with those children. "He's made so many friends here this summer."

Mason nodded. "He fits right in." He looked her way. "And so do you. Come dance with me, Lila." Holding out his hand, he waited for her to take it.

She slipped her hand into his as they moved out onto the dance floor, where a slow song had just begun to play.

Mason drew her into his arms. "I think you forgot to remove your shoes."

"I didn't forget," she said, laughing softly. "I just don't feel like chasing Grits in and out of the festival goers to get my shoe back."

"Ahh, makes sense." They swayed back and forth to the music. "You know he only does that because he likes you. We males do those kind of things when a female has caught our eye. One of the reasons I used to let you win our peach-picking contests."

With a gasp, Lila leaned back to meet his teasing gaze. "*You* let me win? I thought we already concluded that the reason I won was because Jake helped me to beat you."

"Truth be told, my brother suggested that one sure way to keep a girl, you in particular, was to let her win. Although, looking back now, I have to wonder what made me think my little brother had any knowledge of winning a girl's heart. He'd never even dated," he muttered, shaking his head with a grin.

"He might not have had any romantic experience, but that didn't keep your brother from playing matchmaker," Lila said. "Because you're not the only one he was giving advice to."

Mason lifted a questioning brow as they swayed to the music. "No?"

She shook her head. "Jake suggested to me that one sure way to make you want to keep me around was to impress you with my peach-picking skills. He even helped me practice when you went into town. When he saw how poor of a peach picker I really was when I had to do so quickly, he came up with the plan to give me some of his whenever we competed. If I had known you were going to let me win anyway, I wouldn't have gone to all the trouble of—"

"Cheating?" he supplied with a chuckle.

"More of a slight-of-hand trick," she countered.

Their shared laughter filled the air around them, blending into the music coming from the speakers.

Several upbeat dance songs played before Lila found herself drawn back in Mason's arms. She closed her eyes, trying to take in the moment. Not wanting to let him go.

"I love you, Lila."

She looked up into Mason's tender gaze. "I love you, too."

The music stopped, putting an end to their sweet moment.

"Your attention, please," Reverend Hutchins announced, bringing the remaining chatter throughout the festival to a stop, as well. Everyone turned toward the microphone that had been set up for festival announcements, where Reverend Hutchins now stood. "I'm happy to announce that we've raised far more than we'd hoped for today thanks to each and every one of you. I'd like to thank Constance Landers for her generous donation of her family's time, her home, their family business, and for raising such fine children. All of them have volunteered for our church's missionary program many, many times over. Constance has supported their need to spread the word of God through these mission trips, just as she will be doing again when her son leaves for the Democratic Republic of the Congo next month. Please keep her son in your prayers during his travels. Now, I'd like for the Landers family to join me up front so that their generosity and selfless sacrifices might be recognized."

Mason looked to Lila.

"Go on," she said with a smile, despite the unshed tears shimmering in her eyes.

Nodding, he stepped toward the edge of the dance floor to join his family alongside the reverend. The crowd that had gathered on the dance floor and in the surrounding yard quickly swallowed Mason up.

He loved her. Twice he'd spoken those words to her in the past week or so. While that made her heart weep with joy every bit as it had the first time, it also made his going even harder to take. His determination to put his life in what could be a dangerous situation was as admirable as it was terrifying. He had to come back to her. To Finn. And if he could be strong, so could she.

She would busy herself during his time

away to search for a teaching position in, or close to, Sweet Springs. And if she had to wait until the next school year for that to happen, she would find some other job to support her and Finn until something came through. She knew for certain she wouldn't be able to go back to Alabama and start working in September. That meant she needed to let her school know so they would have time to find a replacement for her.

As the chatter around her moved to Mason and his upcoming mission trip, with several people around her discussing their concern for his safety, Lila's own fears for Mason amplified. Did she finally have him back in her life now, only to lose him forever so soon? Surely the Lord would be watching over him.

Fearing an emotional breakdown right there in the middle of the dance floor, Lila turned and wove her way through the crowd. Once off the dance floor, she headed for the orchard. Toward the peace she'd always found there. Maybe there she would be able to calm her racing thoughts. So much had happened over the past week. Mason's admission that he loved her. His asking her to consider moving back. Last-minute preparations for the festival. Her decision to move back to Sweet Springs and the mental planning she'd been doing to make it happen. And then that day's reality of how soon Mason would be leaving on his mission trip and the risks he could face. No wonder her head was spinning.

Walking until she came to her and Mason's special tree, Lila settled beneath it, her back resting against its trunk. Drawing up her knees, she wrapped her arms around them and stared off into the rows of recently harvested peach trees. She felt close to Mason when she was here, because it was so much a part of him. This was where she would come while he was away on his mission trip. Maybe even write her thoughts down in a journal as she had when she was a young girl.

She would miss Mason so much. So would Finn. Closing her eyes, she sent a prayer heavenward for Mason's safekeeping, grateful that she had her faith to see her through the months ahead.

After the reverend's announcement, Mason went in search of Lila, who was no longer waiting for him on the dance floor. When he didn't find her among the throng of people milling about outside the market, he headed inside to look for her there. It was possible she had gotten called away.

"Mason," Mrs. Tully greeted with a smile

from behind the checkout counter, "I was so happy to hear that we've raised the money needed for your upcoming trip."

He nodded. "We had a great turnout today, helping to reach our goal much faster than previous years. But I won't be receiving the money raised, Jake will."

"I'm sorry?" she replied, blinking in confusion.

"My brother has offered to take my place on this mission trip," he explained, keeping his voice low so that only Mrs. Tully would hear. He didn't want Lila to learn of the change from someone other than himself. Wanted to see her smile when she heard that he wouldn't be leaving after all. "He said my place is here in the States with my family."

"I'm sure Lila and Finn would love nothing more, but can you do that?" she asked. "I would think that everything is already set in place."

"Jake already checked into the possibility of this being done should I agree to his taking my place when he spoke with me. Reverend Hutchins told him they could make it work with a few minor adjustments. Therefore, I've decided to accept his offer and remain here instead with the woman I love and focus on my family."

"Bless that boy," his neighbor replied, moisture filling her eyes. "Your little brother really has grown into a fine young man."

"Speaking of my family, have you seen Lila?" he asked, glancing around.

"Not since she left with you to go dance."

"Okay, I'll go look around outside again. I must have missed her."

"Easy to do with so many people in attendance," she agreed.

He met the older woman's kind gaze. Lila had no family other than Finn. This woman was the only real mother Lila had ever known. He found himself glad that he hadn't found Lila first. Smiling, he said, "I'm going to ask Lila to marry me."

Mrs. Tully gasped, her eyes lighting up, "You are?"

"I am," he said quietly, determined to keep their conversation between them alone. "I love her, and since you are the closest thing she has to a momma, I would really like to have your blessing when I ask her to become my wife."

She bobbed her head up and down, her eyes thick with unshed tears. "I couldn't ask for a better man to be her husband."

His smile widened. "So I have your blessing?"

"You have it."

"Thank you, Mrs. Tully. That means a lot."

"Mama Tully to you," she said, beaming with happiness. "Since we're going to be family and all."

"Mama Tully," he repeated. "Now, I'll go see about getting myself into your family." Turning, he walked away. Once outside the market, Mason stopped and glanced around, trying to spot that blond curl-filled ponytail among the sea of heads. Not an easy feat considering Lila's petite height. He was eager to find her, to tell her of the unexpected change in his plans.

"Hey, Daddy."

Mason turned to find Finn standing there, a fluff of half-eaten blue spun candy on a stick clutched in his raised hand. "Looks like somebody's enjoying the festivities."

His son nodded with a grin.

"I was looking for your momma. Have you seen her?"

Finn shook his head. "Not since she was dancing with you."

"I saw her head into the orchard toward Vera Tully's place." A woman spoke up behind him.

Turning, he offered a nod of greeting. "Mrs. Sloane."

She offered up a warm smile. "She left

right after the reverend called you and your family to join him to be recognized."

"Thank you," he said, finding it odd that she hadn't waited for him to return for her. "She must have run home to get something." It was getting a bit cooler as the sun was going down. But still, he worried. Had something been said to Lila that had made her want to step away from the festivities? He prayed not. He wanted this evening to be perfect. Needed it to be. This was his and Lila's second chance to grab onto the future together they had dreamed of.

"I hope she gets back before the sun sets," she said. "I don't think the moon's going to make an appearance tonight. Not with the clouds that have rolled in. The orchard will be too dark to walk through then. Although I suppose she could drive over if need be."

"I'll make sure she makes it back to the festival safely," he assured her with a forced smile. What if Lila had taken ill? She hadn't seemed under the weather when they'd been dancing. Although he had seen a shimmer of unshed tears in her eyes when the reverend called for Mason and his family to join him. He'd put it down to her being happy that all their hard work had come to fruition, raising more money than any of them had expected. Had he been wrong?

"I'll let you go on your way," Mrs. Sloane said. "I'm off to try and win one of those beautiful baskets your momma and the other women put together."

Mason stood watching her go, although his thoughts were elsewhere. Back to Lila and the tears he'd seen shimmering in her eyes before he'd gone to join his family as the reverend had requested. Tears that had come after his profession of love. Had they been tears of joy? Or had his heartfelt words sent her running again? Was that why she'd left the festival?

No, he thought with a mental head shake, she wouldn't have left without Finn. She wouldn't have run away…again. Not when they were so close to having the future they both longed for.

"Want a bite?"

Pulled from his thoughts, Mason glanced down at his son, who had raised his stick of cotton candy in offer. Blue-tinted lips framed his smile, sticky evidence of his thorough enjoyment of his treat. "Looks tasty, but my belly is full up from all the pizza I've eaten."

With a shrug, Finn ripped another piece of sugary fluff off for himself, shoving it into his mouth.

It struck Mason that Finn had only known one parent for all his life until now. Adding another person to that family unit was a big change, even if Finn had voiced his desire to be a part of Mason's life. After a quick glance around to make certain no one was close enough to hear their conversation, he knelt in front of his son. "How would you feel about my asking your momma to marry me?"

Finn's eyes widened, those blue lips rounding into an O. "For real?" he asked.

"For real," Mason said with a chuckle.

"And we'd all live together?"

"That's the plan." He just prayed that he'd be able to find Lila and that she would be as excited as he was at the thought of their getting married and finally becoming a real family.

With a whoop of joy, his son launched himself at Mason.

Reacting on instinct, Mason opened his arms just in time to receive Finn's exuberant hug. That was all the answer he needed. After the hug ended, Mason said, "I'm going to go find your momma and ask her. I hope she's as excited as you are."

"She will be," his son said. "I heard her tell Gramma Tully that she never stopped loving you."

Mason's heart swelled. Lila had told him the same thing, but to know she'd shared that truth with the woman she thought of as a mother really brought it home. Theirs was a love that had survived time and distance, hurt and betrayal, and then forgiveness, growing stronger. "We'll come find you later." He just prayed it would be with good news, because he would hate to think that he gotten his son's hopes up only to have them crushed by Lila's possibly turning him down. But his heart told him Lila felt the same way he did.

Mason set off through the orchard, taking the main path Lila and he used to go back and forth between his place and Mama Tully's. He was about halfway to his destination when he came across Lila sitting beneath their tree, knees drawn up, arms wrapped around them. Her face was lowered, but that didn't keep the sound of soft sobs from reaching him.

"Lila?" he called out as he moved toward her.

Her head snapped up. "Mason?" she said with a startled gasp.

He knelt beside her. "What's wrong?" Then his worried gaze swept over her. "Are you hurt?"

"No," she said, shaking her head.

"Then why are you crying?"

"I hadn't meant to," she said. "I came here

to pray for you. This was always our special place, so it seemed like the place I needed to be to open up my heart to God. I asked God to keep you safe while you're away in the Congo, but when I got to the part where I was telling Him that I couldn't bear the thought of possibly losing you again—forever—the tears just came."

Wrapping an arm around her shoulders, he said, "I thank you for caring so deeply. That means more to me than you could ever know. But you might send up a prayer for Jake's safety instead."

She looked up at him. "Jake?"

He nodded. "My brother has offered to go on the mission trip in my place so that I can stay here with my family."

"He did?"

"He did."

"That's so kind of him."

"I think he had ulterior motives," he said with a grin. "Being the matchmaker he is and all." That said, he shifted into a kneeling position and dug a hand into the front pocket of his pants. "So I'm going to do my part to make his sacrifice for us worth it."

"Mason," she said, her hand coming to her mouth. Fresh tears slid down her cheeks.

"Lila," he replied as he opened the ring

box he'd pulled from his pocket, "you are, and have always been, the other half of my heart. I want you in my life. I want us to be the family we were always meant to be—you, me and Finn. I want to build a house for our family to grow in. I want to get a dog and train it to bring your shoes to you instead of having to come to your shoes' rescue over and over again."

"That would be really nice," she said with a soft giggle.

"Not that I mind being your shoe-rescuing hero," he clarified and then grew serious. "But I want to be so much more. I want to be the one you turn to when times are tough. The one who makes you laugh. Let me be your strength, your anchor, the other half of your heart. And let me be the father to our son I long to be." Pulling the ring from its cushiony nest inside the tiny velvet jewelry box, he said, "This is the ring I intended to give you nine years ago."

"You've kept it all these years?" she gasped in surprise.

"I did," he replied with a nod. "I could never bring myself to let it go. Just as my heart refused to let you go. I thank God for bringing you back into my life. For giving us this second chance."

"Me, too," she said softly.

"I love you, Lila Gleeson. Will you do me the honor of becoming my wife?" His gaze came to rest on the simple solitaire ring as he held it up between them. "I know the diamond's a bit on the small side. It's all I could afford at that age. But we can change it out."

"No," she said, shaking her head. "It's perfect the way it is." Her teary gaze lifted to meet his. "God is good. Through Him, I've found the happiness I've spent my entire lifetime searching for. You have all of my heart, Mason Landers. For now and always. So, to answer your question, yes, I would love very much to marry you."

"For now and always," he said as he slid the ring onto her finger. Then, cupping her face, he bent to press a tender kiss to her lips. A promise of a future filled with love.

* * * * *

Dear Reader,

I'm so excited to be able to share Mason and Lila's emotional journey to happiness with all my readers. It's about trying to do what's right and realizing down the road that you had other options—better options. And how those choices you made affected not only your but so many other lives. It's about forgiveness and working to rebuild broken hearts and mend relationships. *With All Her Heart* also touches on the bond that started between two young girls, Lila and Addy, who first came together as foster sisters and have built a friendship that has continued into adulthood. We discover their long-kept secret and feel the guilt that secret has caused them. A truth that changes so many lives. And we also see how, through faith, those hurts can be overcome and finally allow Mason, Lila and their son, Finn, to be the family they were always meant to be.

Kat

Get 4 FREE REWARDS!

We'll send you 2 FREE Books plus 2 FREE Mystery Gifts.

Love Inspired Suspense books showcase how courage and optimism unite in stories of faith and love in the face of danger.

FREE Value Over $20

Get 4 FREE REWARDS!

We'll send you 2 FREE Books plus 2 FREE Mystery Gifts.

Harlequin Heartwarming Larger-Print books will connect you to uplifting stories where the bonds of friendship, family and community unite.

FREE Value Over $20

THE WESTERN HEARTS COLLECTION!

19 FREE BOOKS in all!

COWBOYS. RANCHERS. RODEO REBELS.
Here are their charming love stories in one prized Collection:
51 emotional and heart-filled romances that capture the majesty and rugged beauty of the American West!

YES! Please send me **The Western Hearts Collection** in Larger Print. This collection begins with 3 FREE books and 2 FREE gifts in the first shipment. Along with my 3 free books, I'll also get the next 4 books from The Western Hearts Collection, in LARGER PRINT, which I may either return and owe nothing, or keep for the low price of $5.45 U.S./$6.23 CDN each plus $2.99 U.S./$7.49 CDN for shipping and handling per shipment*. If I decide to continue, about once a month for 8 months I will get 6 or 7 more books but will only need to pay for 4. That means 2 or 3 books in every shipment will be FREE! If I decide to keep the entire collection, I'll have paid for only 32 books because 19 books are FREE! I understand that accepting the 3 free books and gifts places me under no obligation to buy anything. I can always return a shipment and cancel at any time. My free books and gifts are mine to keep no matter what I decide.

☐ 270 HCN 5354   ☐ 470 HCN 5354

Name (please print)

Address   Apt. #

City   State/Province   Zip/Postal Code

Mail to the **Reader Service:**
IN U.S.A.: P.O. Box 1341, Buffalo, N.Y. 14240-8531
IN CANADA: P.O. Box 603, Fort Erie, Ontario L2A 5X3